DEAD WEDNESDAY

JERRY SPINELLI

Alfred A. Knopf
New York

THIS IS A BORZOI BOOK PUBLISHED BY ALFRED A. KNOPF

All rights reserved. Published in the United States by Alfred A. Knopf, an imprint of Random House Children's Books, a division of Penguin Random House LLC, New York.

Knopf, Borzoi Books, and the colophon are registered trademarks of Penguin Random House LLC.

Visit us on the Web! rhcbooks.com

Educators and librarians, for a variety of teaching tools, visit us at RHTeachersLibrarians.com

Library of Congress Cataloging-in-Publication Data is available upon request.
ISBN 978-0-593-30667-3 (trade) — ISBN 978-0-593-30668-0 (lib. bdg.) —
ISBN 978-0-593-30669-7 (ebook)

The text of this book is set in 11.2-point Gamma ITC Std.
Interior design by Cathy Bobak

Printed in the United States of America
August 2021
10 9 8 7 6 5 4 3 2 1
First Edition

To Kathy Frazier
and the Stargirls
of Kent, Ohio

That it will never come again
Is what makes life so sweet.

—Emily Dickinson

THE NINTH OF JUNE
aka
DEAD WEDNESDAY

No way.

This is Worm's first groggy thought even before he opens his eyes. He actually whispers it to his pillow: "No way." Because the feeling he wakes up with—the same one he went to bed with—makes no sense: he wants to go to school.

Wants to!

But now—eyes open, head clearing—he realizes it's true. For the first time in his life, he *does* want to go to school. He deliciously reviews the reasons:

1. It's a half day—hah!—*if* . . .

2. . . . *if* you're an eighth grader. Then you get to motorize on outta there at the end of fourth period. That's 11:43 if you're keeping score. And OMG, does it get any better? . . . Even though he'll be *there*, it'll be like he's *not there*. Think it

3

again, Worm: *like he's not there.* Why? Because of this dumb, gorgeous thing called Dead Wednesday. He's been hearing it since his elementary days: if you're an eighth grader, you get to be invisible. In the past two years he's witnessed it. No teacher will ask you a question. Nobody will hassle you. You can goof off all you want and nobody will care. Worm has witnessed Frisbees and moose calls flying in the hallways. Eddie himself has said many times: "You can stand on the teacher's desk and blow a rocket blastoff fart, and you won't get sent to Discipline."

Worm doesn't doubt Eddie. But neither does he care much about the license to goof off. To begin with, he's not a goof-offer. Plus, he *likes* the part about being invisible. For Worm is well named. He prefers to be out of sight, underground, watching, listening. A spectator. *He walked the world unseen.* That would be Worm's perfect epitaph. He mouths a silent thank-you to the Wrappers.

3. Every minute spent in school brings the end of it closer. Seven days and a wake-up. And then comes the only thing that makes the nine and a half months of school endurable: the ocean, the prairie, the vast Siberia of schoolless time known as summer vacation.

So yeah . . . today . . . today he *wants* to go to school.

Oh . . . and how could he forget?

4. The fight. Jeep Waterstone and Snake Davis are going to fight at twelve-thirty at the old cannon in Veterans Park.

4

They've hated each other since first grade and they're finally going to settle it.

So Worm has awakened to a day like no other, a day of four beautiful things. He stretches in bed, reviews the beautiful things in his mind. . . .

Every Thanksgiving, when two grandmas and a grandpa show up, Worm's father stands over the turkey and smothers everybody in a stupid grin and shakes his head as if he can't believe it and says, "We are truly blessed." Until that moment passes, Worm is always a tight knot of cringe. But now, for the first time, he gets it. He *is* blessed.

Worm's pj bottoms are down at his knees when his bedroom door begins to open. He screams, "Mom!"

The door slams shut.

"You're never up!" she screams back.

"Well, I'm up today!"

"You're *never* up!"

"I'm *up*!"

"Every morning I have to drag you out of bed"—he can tell by her receding voice that she's heading back down the hallway—"every morning of your *life*. . . ."

Did she see him?

He doesn't think so. He caught a glimpse of her chin and fingers at the edge of the door, but no eye.

He quickly fumbles out of his pj's and into his clothes.

As he's pulling on his sneaks, he wonders how many will show up at the fight. All the guys, he figures. And some girls. Shoot—maybe even a teacher or two!

He tugs his laces tight. He smiles. He allows himself a little giggle. He whispers to his sneaks: "I am truly blessed."

The blessing abruptly ends as Worm walks the plank.

That's what it feels like: down the hallway, past his parents' bedroom, down the stairs, through the dining room. Only it's not a normal dining room. People are already there—strangers—sitting at two round tables, eating breakfast, his mother smiling a whole year's worth, shamelessly kissing butts. "More coffee, Mr. So-and-So?" "Is the toast warm enough, Miss So-and-So?"

The strangers in his house are writers. They stay in eight cabins in the meadow (which Worm has to mow). Most of them take their meals in his dining room. The rest of the time they're in the cabins, writing away.

His parents advertise it online:

WRITERS' RE-TREAT!
Just YOU and your MANUSCRIPT
in the
BEAUTY and SOLITUDE
of the
POCONO MOUNTAINS!

Every morning Worm dreads the endless walk through the dining room. He hates it as much as he hates mirrors. He cannot believe he once looked forward to it.

His mother claims that when he was really little, he used to entertain the dining room writers by singing "I'm a Little Teapot" for them, complete with adorable gestures. Worm has no memory of this, and the older he gets, the more he doubts it's true.

What he does remember is his mother introducing him to each week's new batch of writers:

"This is our son, Robbie. You can thank him for your fresh towels each day."

Followed by a blitz:

"Hi, Robbie!"

"Hi, Robbie!"

"Hi, Robbie!"

Things came to a head one day a year ago when his mother roadblocked him and introduced him to some

9

supposedly famous writer of books for kids: "Robbie, this is Gwen Nevins." To Worm's horror, the lady put down her fork, wiped her mouth with a napkin, and stood as if Worm was some big shot or something. "Robbie," she said, "nice to meet you," and stuck out her hand. Worm heard his mother say, "Robbie devours your books."

Worm sent her his Look of Surprise. "Do I?" he said, and gave the writer's hand a limp fish and escaped into the kitchen.

His mother never introduced him again.

Now, on this second Wednesday in June, he practically sprints through the dining room and almost makes it before some old lady quacks, "Hi there, young man!" He sends his signature response—a quick up-flip of his hand—and he's into the kitchen.

He feels his daily microsecond of relief—and then, as always, it's gone. For all he's done is go from one stage to another, one spotlight to another.

Worm doesn't consider himself a hater. You have to care to hate. You have to give a crap. And frankly, there's not a whole lot Worm gives a crap about. But there is one thing he does hate with a passion, maybe even more than school: he hates being the center of attention. In the spotlight.

"He's just shy," his mother has said to people a thousand

times, explaining his behavior. Worm is sure there's a better word out there, but he hasn't found it. He knows why he's shy these days, to the point where it's hard to believe he's ever been anything but. And even though he increasingly believes his mother is lying about him performing "I'm a Little Teapot," he sometimes curls himself around a secret he can't tell: he kind of likes it. It weirdly fascinates him to think he might have once been different. Whatever happened to that little teapot?

The kitchen is just slightly better than the dining room.

Worm's father looks up from his coffee with a face that can only be described as thrilled. "The Wormster!" he belts. Worm responds in his usual way: he doesn't. Which, as usual, does nothing to slow down the runaway train of his father. "Seven days and a wake-up!" His dad has talked calendar like this since he was in army boot camp, counting the days. "Gimme a *W* . . . gimme an *O*. . . ." Worm sits down at the table, chugs his orange juice in the hope that looking occupied will divert the attention. It doesn't. "Who says worms are slow?"

Worm's nightmare: someday when he enters a room, his father is going to jump up and clap, cheer, whistle, and throw confetti. He was a cheerleader in college.

12

Dining room, kitchen. This is why Worm hates—maybe he *is* a hater—school-day mornings.

And why he'll be celebrating this time next week. Two and a half months of sleeping in, deleting all this from his life. There's no spotlight in bed.

But to be fair, fatherwise, Worm understands. He knows his dad isn't really ragging on him. It's just the way he is: wordy, smiley. He can't help himself. Before he and Mom started the writers' retreat, he was a salesman. Office products. Now in his spare time he acts in plays at the Barleycorn Playhouse. And to his credit, how many fathers would call their kid Worm?

To his mother's credit, she at least treats him more like a regular human being than a star of stage, screen, and writers' retreats. This morning, glory be, she even apologizes to him. "Robbie, honey. Sorry I snapped at you up there. I was just so surprised . . . you usually—"

"No problem," he says. Says it in a way that kills any oncoming speech and sends her to the counter for his cinnamon toast. She lays two slices on his plate. He hurries to butter them while they're still hot. Butter sinking into cinnamon swirl toast. Life is good.

Until she speaks again. "Robbie . . . did you notice anything?"

"Uh . . . no?" he says.

"It's something we're not doing, Dad and I."

"I give up." He's chewing away. Damn if he's going to let his toast get cold while he has a stupid discussion.

"We're not *not* talking to you. We're *not* ignoring you."

How do you respond to something like that? "Thanks," he says mouthfully.

"Dead Wednesday? Ring a bell?"

He hopes his silence, his concentrated chewing, will send the message.

It doesn't.

"Earth to Robbie?"

He gives up. His breakfast is ruined. "It's just a school thing," he points out.

"Well, not totally," his father chips in. He's a master balancer. He always manages to support both his wife and his kid. "It's supposed to be a whole-town thing."

Worm knows this, but he has no intention of getting into a debate about it. He stands up, grabs his backpack, remembers he won't need it today, figures, *OK, you wanna play that game . . .* , pointedly dumps his backpack on the floor, pointedly neglects to go brush his teeth. If he's invisible, so are his teeth and backpack.

Of course she won't let it go. "I know parents who say they're going to ignore their kids all day long. Starting at breakfast."

"That's stupid," he says. He doesn't believe it . . . and wonders who.

14

"It's about safety, honey. Growing up. Responsibility."

"It's bull . . ." He says it in a way that tells them they're lucky he's leaving off the back half of the word.

He's almost tempted to hang around and watch the look on their faces. He heads out the kitchen door, his father calling, "You da Worm!"

For four minutes every school day, Worm is king of the world. It's the only benefit he can think of to living so far out in the boondocks. He's the school bus's first stop. And last coming back. For four minutes it's just him and the driver.

There are reasons why Worm likes being first get-on and last get-off:

1. Nobody can see where he lives. Prehistoric farmhouse. Eight Abe Lincoln log cabins. Old outhouse converted to toolshed that still looks like old outhouse. Woods. Black bears. Caterpillars the size of fingers.

2. For four minutes he gets to pretend he's a superrich kid being chauffeured around in the world's longest limo.

3. He has (on the morning ride into school, at least) the whole busful of seats to pick from. He always sits in

16

the second-to-last row, by the window on the left side. He doesn't worry about the seat beside him. Everybody knows it's Eddie's.

4. For four minutes he gets to watch and think. That's how Worm sees himself: as a watcher-thinker. *(The Worm Knows All.)* Probably because he's an only child living in the boondocks; what else is there to do? Every day he looks forward to sighting his first human. (Parents and retreating writers don't count.) He experiences daily something denied to kids who live in town: the mini thrill of entering civilization.

But not today.

7:26 a.m.

Today Worm has barely settled into his seat when he
hears the *ping* in his pocket. Text. Mother.

> Sorry . . . forgot . . . you have to come
> straight home today when they let you
> out. Just take the bus.

He almost laughs. This is an easy one:

> no

Her: No choice. No argument. Sorry.
And miss a free half day in town with Eddie? Miss the
fight? Seriously?

no

Her: Robbie! I need you here!! Dad will be away!!

Him: where

Her: Aunt Rita. Helping her move.

Him: i have plans

Her: Sorry! I'll make it up to you. I triple dog promise! YOU MUST!!!

Him: no

He kills the cell, stuffs it in his pocket.

Texting upside: easier to say no. Texting downside: they can always reach you.

His mother is actually doing it, glooming up a perfect day. The speech at breakfast—she's got him feeling guilty (slightly) for thanking the Wrappers as he got out of bed this morning.

The bus stops for kid number two: Stephanie Win. His four minutes are over.

Seven more stops, and now . . .

. . . Forrest Avenue.

No stop. No slowing down. No pointing. No indication that anyone realizes what a special line they are crossing. But Worm knows. Forrest Avenue is the northern boundary of Amber Springs.

Town.

Every day the street sign reminds him how badly he wants to live on the other side of Forrest. In town. Civilization. At every stop from now on, he will envy the kids who board the bus. They don't know how lucky they are.

Up and down the bus you can tell the eighth graders at a glance: no backpacks. No need for them today.

A muted *ping* in his pocket. What did he expect—his mom would give up? Worm sticks his tongue out and quickly withdraws it. It's an embarrassing leftover habit

20

from his little-kid days. Worm was one of the last boys in his grade to get the low voice. He likes girls, but unlike Eddie and other hunks and Romeos, he has had no real experience with them. He knows he trails the pack in the maturity race. He also knows that's one reason why he likes to hang with Eddie. With Eddie he feels a little older, a little more manly, than when he's alone.

At Noble Street a skeleton gets on. Walks the full length of the bus for max exposure.

It's David Ott. Nobody else would wear a skeleton suit for Dead Wed.

Guys along the aisle fist-bump him, say stuff:

"Otter."

"Yo, Otter."

"Killin' it, man."

The skeleton is cool, slow, doesn't speak. The girls are going bananas. Meanwhile, the bus is grumbling at idle, waiting for the skeleton to sit. And now some girls pop up, chanting, "Ot-*ter!* Ot-*ter!*" Laughing, cheering, even a whistle. Which makes the ever-grouchy driver swing around, point, growl: "Down! Sit! Now!"

It occurs to Worm to call out: *Skeletons don't need to sit!* But he doesn't. He thinks a lot of things he doesn't say. *Shy.* His tag. Never got to "I'm a *Big* Teapot." By now his old nickname and more recent tag have publicly merged: *Worm. Shy.* For the most part it discourages people from trying to lure him from the sidelines to join the scrum. *Don't ask Worm. He's shy.*

Skeleton passing, fist bump:

"Worm."

"Otter."

The skeleton takes a seat in the back. Worm wonders how long Otter will get away with it. The bus lurches.

Next stop: Monica Biddle. She always sits in a front seat. She never looks at him. It wasn't always that way. She used to sit toward the back, a couple of seats in front of Worm. Then one morning last year, in seventh grade, she paused before sitting down and stared directly into his eyes and said, loud enough for others to hear, "Get a life, Worm."

Since then he's been trying to figure it out. Why did she say it? What did he do?

After a year he's come up with a guess: she said it because, as Shy Worm, he may in fact appear to have no life. Which doesn't mean Monica Biddle should announce it to the universe. Every day when she boards the bus, he wants to scream at her: *I do have a life! You just can't see it!*

One of the things she can't see is his favorite daydream, which features himself—as a real worm—crawling up her nose, preferably at dinnertime in front of her horrified parents.

Ah . . . Eddie's stop.

8:09 a.m.

Eddie's on, heading down the aisle. The world is right again.

Worm stares out the window, doesn't look at Eddie. He's always careful not to show how thrilled he is to see his best pal. Feeling Eddie sit beside him, he swings his right arm, offers his fist, feels the bump.

"Yo."

"Yo."

Eddie settles in, and first thing, sure enough, he says, "Pathetic."

It's Eddie's signature word: *pathetic.* Worm hears him use it at least a couple of times a day. It's become a handy way for Worm to evaluate his environment, to learn what's cool and what's not. When Eddie pronounces something or someone "pathetic," another pixel in Worm's world goes to high-def.

Worm immediately seeks the target of Eddie's eyes. It's a kid just now bumbling late onto the bus. As the kid wobbles down the aisle, Worm studies him . . . why the "pathetic"? . . . Ah, now he sees it: the belt. The kid, no doubt a sixth grader who doesn't know any better, is wearing a belt that belongs in either a museum or a dumpster. It's covered in little beads: black for the background and clusters of orange beads that form a parade of jack-o'-lanterns around his waist. Breaking news, runt: Halloween is four months away.

Eddie often gives sixth graders a pass, but Worm understands why this cannot be overlooked. The kid finds a seat, totally unaware that he's been defined and boxed by the captain of the bus. Worm loves being on the good side of "pathetic."

One thing about *shy* (Worm) and *cool* (Eddie): the inside stuff may be different, but to others they probably look pretty much the same. Worm knows he'll never *be* cool. He's just glad to get splashed by some of Eddie's cool.

Sometimes he still can't believe it: him and Eddie. Best buds. Besides cool, Eddie is everything else Worm is not: great-looking, popular, athletic, a leader. The skin on his face is smooth as an M&M. He probably doesn't even know what Clearasil is. Girls love him and, in their own way, so do guys. And yet—Worm still can't believe it—they're best friends. Every once in a while he'll hear somebody say, "Eddie and Worm . . . ," and he feels all cotton candy inside.

Every day when Eddie plops down next to him on the bus, he wants to yell up the aisle: *Hey, Mean Monica! Look who Eddie Fusco's sitting next to! Loser!*

When Eddie speaks again, it is, again, one word: "Fight."

Worm turns to him, grins. "Twelve-thirty."

Eddie's response is to punch the seat back in front of him. Jolted, the kid in the seat barks, "Hey!" and turns. When he sees it's Eddie Fusco, he laughs and shoots a thumbs-up. "Hey, Eddie."

"So," says Worm, "who do you think, Jeep or Snake?"

Eddie mulls it over. "Hard to say. They're both nasty. Better be an ambulance ready."

"Think girls'll come?"

Eddie snorts. "Girls? How about *teachers*?"

They fist-bump.

"And then what?" says Worm.

"What when?" says Eddie.

"After the fight. What're we gonna do then?"

Eddie nods. "Gotta make it count." The free day, he means.

"Gotta," says Worm.

"I'll think about it."

"Cool," says Worm.

Worm considers the amazingness of it all. "Dead Wed, man."

Eddie makes his hands like a prayer, looks up at the ceiling of the bus. "Thank you, Wrappers."

That's what they call the kids whose deaths make this a holiday for eighth graders every year. It comes from newspaper descriptions of teenage drivers zooming around curves at night and sailing off the road and wrapping their cars and themselves and their passengers around telephone poles or trees. Car accidents in particular and deaths in general come in many other ways, but the tag has stuck, and good luck now trying to pry it off. *Wrappers.*

Hearing Eddie say this, Worm feels better about silently thanking the Wrappers earlier. In fact, he figures the backpackless eighth graders up and down the bus are all thinking the same thing: *Thank you, Wrappers.* Like, c'mon, who doesn't secretly want to jump on a teacher's desk and detonate a rocket blastoff fart or two? The point is being *allowed* to. Even if you really wouldn't.

Worm is feeling it: his best pal beside him . . . fight at the cannon . . . Dead Wed. It comes to him that the full force of becoming a teenager did not hit him on his recent fourteenth birthday, but today, now. He doesn't think the words, they simply pop out: "Perfect day."

28

At first it seems Eddie doesn't hear him. Now suddenly, in a way only Eddie can do, he bolts up from his seat, throws out his arms like Moses parting the Red Sea, and bellows: "PERFECT DAY!"

The bus erupts. Cheers, whistles. Sixth and seventh graders drop their guard and frolic, tasting eighth grade. The skeleton and a dozen kids jive-rock up and down the aisle. They all fall laughing as the bus lurches to a stop, the driver roaring, "Seats! Now! Delinquents!"

Worm watches, soaks in the honor of being the one who started it all. Eddie took what he said and turned it into magic. Thanks to Worm, the bus driver called them all "delinquents."

Laughing collapsers are crawling to their seats. The cell pings in his pocket. Text. He reads it. Stuffs the cell. His mood sours. "My mother wants me to come right home."

Eddie looks like he's been whacked in the head. He blinks. "Huh? When?"

"Right after. She says take the bus."

On this day every year several buses show up at the end of fourth period, ready to transport freedom-drunk eighth graders home. This year the buses will be running mostly empty. This year kids will be heading for the fight at the cannon.

Eddie's face shows he still doesn't get it. "The fight," he says.

"Don't worry," he tells Eddie. "I ain't doing it." His pocket pings again. He ignores it. "I told her no."

And gets a look from Eddie—an *I'm proud of you, dude* look, a grin, a nod, as if something he's always suspected has been confirmed. Eddie offers his fist, they bump. "My man," Eddie says.

8:16 a.m.

Last stop: Beautiful Bijou Newton gets on.

She's the girl version of Eddie. Perfect. As she steps up and into the bus, a bolt of electricity flies down the aisle. Her time on-bus is a tragically brief four minutes. But there's a blessed upside. In a rare example of boy-girl co-operation, the riders conspire to make sure the one remaining empty seat is always in the back row. Any one of the four will do. What this does is compel Beautiful to walk the entire length of the bus.

The main object, of course, is to give every eyeball a chance to feast up close. But her perfection is more than skin-deep. She's just too darn nice to be jealous of. She's anything but snooty. When the subject of her looks is forced upon her, she does the finger-in-mouth gag thing and mocks herself: "Beautiful schmootiful. You should see me in the morning. You'd call the dogcatcher!" Which only makes her more lovable.

On this Wednesday, like every school day, Beautiful Bijou dispenses hi's and smiles as she glides down the runway.

After she passes them, Eddie leans into Worm and whispers: "She dumped the Hulk."

Worm boggles. "When?"

"Yesterday. After school."

"Whoa."

News does not get bigger than this. Hulk Abernathy, a junior-year all-state tackle in high school, has been going with Beautiful since before Christmas. Two weeks ago they were the centerpiece of the eighth-grade prom. (Or so Worm has heard.) No middle schooler has ever dared to make a move on her. Not even Eddie Fusco.

Normally, Worm would safely process this breaking news from his place on the sideline, but something has happened today that has never happened before. As Beautiful approached them on her walk down the aisle, her smile—usually a sweeping, one-size-fits-all greeting—came briefly to a halt and landed somewhere. Worm will later realize that the landing must have lasted only a moment. But for now it seems to him that time has stopped, and the smile is like a painting forever hanging on a wall. And the reason the whole thing strikes Worm this way is because—contrary to everything he knows about how the universe works—the landing place of Beautiful Bijou's smile seems to have been . . . *himself.*

Into the school driveway. Backpacks climb onto shoulders like pet monkeys. When the kids are bad, like today, the grumpy driver keeps the door shut, punishing them. Within seconds, forty-four kids are crammed into the front half of the aisle. Worm thinks he feels Beautiful Bijou somewhere behind him. Suddenly the door opens. Kids gush out. Worm wants to turn and spot her getting off, but he can't make himself do it.

The mob pours through the school door, but unlike any other day, they don't scatter to homerooms. They're pooled just inside, waiting to see what happens with the skeleton.

Otter doesn't even make it through the door. Mr. Krebs, the vice principal, blocks him and utters a single word: "Off."

A cloudburst of boos as Otter peels off his mask and now the Halloween costume. For a second Worm thinks

34

Otter might be wearing nothing underneath but Fruit of the Looms, which would be historic. But it's only regular clothes. An arms-up Rocky move from the former skeleton and the boos change to cheers, and David Ott leads the student body on to school.

The doorway is empty.

Every day for three years Mrs. Truitt has been stationed at the Homeroom 113 doorway, smiling, greeting everyone by name: "Good morning, Sarah. . . . Good morning, Leah. . . . Good morning, Robbie. . . ."

Not today.

Today Mrs. Truitt is standing at the far side of the room, looking out the window, her hands behind her back, her back to the class.

Like we're not here, thinks Worm.

A glance to the right and there they are, covering the blackboard and spilling over onto the wall: the Wrappers. Poster-size pictures. Faces. Teenagers. Some in color, some black-and-white. This must be new. He's heard of the cards before, but not the poster pictures.

When you're a kid around here, practically from the time you're a baby, you hear about Dead Wednesday and the Wrappers. At first you're clueless and curious. Then for a couple of years you grim down to its solemn message. Then you look forward to it because by now you're sick of being a little kid, and Dead Wed is, as much as anything, your official ticket to big-kidhood. And finally you crave it as much as your favorite junk food, because now you understand what Dead Wednesday really, *really* means: a half day of fun at—of all places—school!

And now that it's actually here, there's a sense of unreality about the whole thing, like that time they had the bomb scare. And something else, something Worm has no name for, something about the teacher's back . . . the kids quiet instead of chattery and rowdy . . . the faces on the blackboard . . .

Ping.

His mother never texts him at school. He better check it.

Daisy Chimes is coming!!!
You MUST be here!!!

He pockets the cell.

And now he notices the inner frame of the doorway. It's draped in black crepe paper.

Room 113 is filled with people but feels empty. Just faces in the seats facing faces on the blackboard.

Worm wonders: *When does the fun start?* He wonders how all this is sitting with Eddie. Hah—dumb question. Eddie is cool with everything.

Worm pulls up the Smile on the little screen behind his eyes. But it won't stay in focus; the faces on the blackboard keep getting in the way. He counts them. There are twenty-three. Same as the number of eighth graders in Home-room 113.

And who is Daisy Chimes?

Dead Wednesday

It began in the old days. Somebody's tenth grader took three friends joyriding at 100 mph around the Eagle Mountain curve and smack into an evergreen. Closed caskets for all four.

So they decided that the kids of Amber Springs needed a big-time warning before plunging into the evils of young adulthood.

Before sinking out of reach.

Before high school.

The way it goes, on the second Wednesday in June every eighth grader gets a card with the name of some kid from Pennsylvania who died during the past year. The deaths have to be from something "preventable." Drugs. Alcohol. DAT (driving and texting). MOWD (making out while driving). Recklessness. Unavoidable accidents don't count. Fatal illness doesn't count.

You get something besides the card. You get a black shirt. From the moment you put on the black shirt, it's like you're not yourself, you're the name on the card. You're that kid. You're dead. Teachers don't see you. That's why you can do anything you want.

You're known as a Deader.

But it doesn't stop there. Every household and business in Amber Springs has gotten a flyer in the mailbox explaining Dead Wednesday and asking for cooperation "for the precious futures of our young people." Posters proclaim it from telephone poles and storefront windows along Pocono Street. The "dead" are supposed to wear their black shirts until they go to bed that night.

A surprising number of townspeople go along with it. Walk up to the window at Homer's Water Ice in a black shirt and you might not get served. There are even radical parents who refuse to speak to their kids, even at the dinner table. Worm's mother wasn't lying.

The eighth graders themselves? Sure, some of them are serious. You can see the scared in their eyes. But it's the jokers who steal the show. For Worm, Dead Wed in sixth and seventh grade meant a front-row seat at a circus or comedy club. Farting and belching up and down the hallways. Eighth graders walking out of a room halfway through class.

Or walking clear out of school, usually to return because it's too much fun inside.

Underclassmen have to mind their shoes around water fountains; it's become practically a sacred duty of Deaders when they take a drink at a fountain to spit it out on the floor. It's become a tradition for the class clown to do something really special. Worm wonders what Otter has in mind.

At the end of fourth period most Deaders have to be *kicked* out of school, it's so much fun. By the time they hit the sidewalk, half of them have torn off their black shirts and dumped them in a trash can or in the gutter.

The payoff is supposed to start the next day, Thursday. After being dead for a day, you're supposed to be scared straight. You're supposed to say no to all that bad high school stuff. Yeah, right. Like Dead Wed is going to stop you from having a beer. Not that Worm is into beer or drugs or any vice but his beloved *Nuke 'Em ALL Now!* video game, if you want to call that a vice.

And anyway, who ever heard of a reckless worm?

8:29 a.m.

Time drips like a slowly leaking faucet. Worm ticks off all the things that are not happening. . . .

Not: Mrs. Truitt closing the door, facing the room with her arms out like a group hug, and belting, "Good morning, ladies and gentlemen!" It's corny, but the kids secretly love it and always send back a boisterous "Good morning, dear teacher!" And then she takes the roll, and then she updates them on the latest escapades of her twin toddlers, Amy and Ashton. The Masters of Disaster, she calls them.

Not today.

Not: The vice principal's voice coming through the ancient speaker box above the blackboard, leading them in the Pledge of Allegiance. Through the open door Worm can hear seventh graders reciting the pledge in the homeroom across the hall. But the speaker in room 113 is mute.

Otter, three seats ahead of Worm, can't take it anymore. He stands, plants his hand over his heart, and begins, "I pledge allegiance to the flag . . . ," then collapses, giggling, into his seat. Mrs. Truitt doesn't seem to notice.

Not: Announcements. They should be coming now: what's going on today, who needs to be where, all that. A voice in Worm's head fills in for the vice principal: *Fight . . . twelve-thirty today . . . all eighth graders . . . at the cannon . . . be there!*

A voice.

"Mrs. Truitt?"

Everyone turns to the back row. It's Claire Meeson, shyer even than Worm, and the most law-abiding of them all, hand in the air, speaking without being called on. "Mrs. Truitt?" she peeps again. "I think maybe the PA is turned off?"

All heads swing to Mrs. Truitt at the window. If she's heard Claire Meeson, she's not showing it. Claire cannot retract her hand fast enough. She's devastated. Her lip quivers. Poor clueless Claire. Worm feels like smacking Mrs. Truitt.

Worm returns his attention to the twenty-three Wrappers. Boys and girls. All seem to be looking at him. Some photo trick. He wants to look away but can't. Most are smiling, no clue they're about to be dead. Worm wonders which one he'll get.

Nothing moves, yet something catches his eye. Two rows over. Mean Monica Biddle. Like everyone else, she's facing the Wrappers, but her eyes are closed and her lips are moving.

His pocket pings. Worm has no intention of answering, but just to give himself a break from all this weirdness, he decides to take a peek:

> You wont have to PLAY dead if you dont come home straight after school.

Reluctantly he gives his mother a point for a funny threat.

8:35 a.m.

The bell rings.

Everyone flinches, but nobody gets up. Well, David Ott—of course—walks to the end of his aisle. But he's joking. He one-eighties, flops back into his seat.

All eighth graders have been told: Stay in your homeroom till you get your black shirt.

Squealing sixth and seventh graders stampede past the black-draped doorway, fascinated eyes gawking at the roomful of Deaders. In time the commotion drains into first-period classrooms . . . doors close along the hallway . . . quiet again.

And now Mrs. Truitt is moving. . . .

She opens the top center drawer of her desk and pulls out a white sheet of paper. Her movements are those of a robot. She does not look at her students. She looks at the

clock above the door . . . waits . . . waits . . . and begins
to read: "'The teacher will call one name per minute. Your
name is under your seat. You may get it now.'"

Worm has heard of various ways of getting your Wrapper's name, but never this one. He's been sitting on it the
whole time. He joins twenty-two hands reaching under
seats. He feels it. He pulls it off, a three-by-five-inch card
that's been taped to the underside of the seat.

He looks at the card. There's information on it, but his
eyes go no farther than the top, the first line, the name:

REBECCA ANN FINCH

The teacher continues: "'When a card name is called,
the student holding that name shall leave the room. In the
hallway you will find a rack of black shirts. Put one on and
proceed to your first-period class. Memorize your card. Become your card. Wear your black shirt for the rest of the
day until you go to bed. Speak to no one. You are dead.'"

Worm feels a chill.

"Donald Thomas Benchley."

Everyone looks at their card. Nobody moves. Now, in the back row, Kathy Wishart gets up and heads for the door. Otter half whispers, "Go, Donald."

Worm can hear hangers sliding on a metal rack outside.

It seemed odd at first when Worm saw that his dead person was a girl. Now it seems less odd, since Kathy Wishart has a boy.

Kathy returns. She's buttoned her black shirt all the way to the top. She has forgotten she's supposed to go on to her first class. Mrs. Truitt says nothing. Otter jabs a finger at the door, barks: "Out, dead one!" Kathy's hand flies to her mouth. She turns and scrams.

"Raven Esther Ortega."

This time it's Nicole Fizzano—Fizz to everybody. True to

her name, she's bubbly. "Yeah!" she pipes, and zips up the aisle, high-fiving along the way.

Worm takes the opportunity to look at the card he's supposed to memorize. There are four lines below Rebecca Ann Finch's name—well, five if you count the nickname:

"Becca"

Age: 17

Hometown: Elwood, Pennsylvania

Cause of death: Auto crash

Personal: Bottles lightning bugs

And one other thing: in the upper right-hand corner of the card, like a postage stamp, a picture of Becca Finch.

Worm is barely aware of the next person leaving to the name of "Melinda Abigail Potts," uttered in Mrs. Truitt's new, atonal GPS voice.

Worm studies the little picture, finds Becca Finch among the posters. He tries to spot signs of drinking or a crashing car or death, but all he sees is a girl, short hair, not blond but not real dark either, big smile for the camera . . . which makes Worm think of Beautiful Bijou on the bus. The dazzling smile has both thrilled and confounded Worm— because girls do not smile at him. Not like that.

It's no big mystery. He knows exactly why: the pimples. Acne. They showed up in sixth grade, about the same time he discovered girls, about the same time he became famously shy. He understands. In a school full of peach-cheeked boys, what girl would want the inflamed, pink-pebbled facescape of a kid doomed to pits and craters? He hates cloudless days. He hates fluorescent lighting. He hates mirrors. He hates getting a haircut. He hates cameras.

And yet—insanely—the Smile seemed to say: *I like what I see.*

"Wilma Sally Krebs." He catches this one after missing several, lost in the Smile.

Now it's Claire Meeson's turn. Otter calls, "You da chick!" No more half whispers. Otter has quickly learned this is a day without penalty. Plus, he loves to rag on Claire Meeson, so timid she's known as Meeson the Meek.

Claire scoots out to the hall. And now something incredible happens. Instead of disappearing like the other Deaders, suddenly here she is, spotlight-shunning Claire Meeson, standing in the doorway, the black crepe paper framing her like a portrait of doom. She's draped the black shirt over her shoulders like a cape. She just stands there, staring at them, a look on her face that is goofily un-Claire-like. She balls her fists and pumps her arms like a cheerleader and yells, "Hip! Hip! Hooray!" and is gone. Worm has heard of something called the Dead Wed Effect. Maybe this is it.

The frosty teacher drones on. . . .

"Murray Grey Olinik.

"Paul DeFord Kappelmeyer.

"Elizabeth Eve Patrick-Quarles."

I like what I see. Worm lowers himself into the thought as he would into a bathtub of warm water, works the thought into a lather, and soaps himself.

"Winsome Helen White.

"Wilson Boyd Billicoe."

Ah . . . Otter. "Finally," he groans, gets up, goes out. Everybody tracks his sounds: shuffling at the rack, finding the right size . . . footsteps . . . door opening across the hall, sixth-grade class . . . Otter's graveyard voice . . . "I'm back from the dead—BOO!" . . . squeals and giggles from the class. Worm would have expected a clap or two from Otter's homeroom, but there is nothing. Worm has seen this coming. Blame it on the posters. The faces of the Wrappers. The teacher's back. Her lifeless voice. Room 113 has become grim city. He wonders when the fun will begin.

The class is getting smaller.

"**Louis Petty Van Dorn.**

"Brittany Grace Fong."

Worm is getting uneasy. Over half the class is gone now, and he's becoming more and more visible. He can't possibly be the last one of all twenty-three.

Can he?

"Katherine Louise Hite."

It's Monica Biddle. Worm's first thought is: *Poor dope. You got screwed twice. First you're dead. Now Mean Monica's got your card.*

But Mean Monica surprises him. She doesn't get up. She just sits there. She's crying! Not quiver-lipping like Claire Meeson, but the real thing: hand to the mouth, sobbing, tears.

Mrs. Truitt mercilessly repeats: "Katherine Louise Hite."

Monica Biddle pushes herself up from her desk and races from the room. Worm can hear her running down the hallway. He may have discovered girls at twelve, but that doesn't mean he understands them. All girl mysteries default to Eddie's one-word-fits-all: *chicks.*

"Morgan Billie Fornance.

"Wilson Robert Schultz."

He wonders how it's going up in 214, Eddie's homeroom.

"Anthony John Ciardi.

"Rachel Eva Morgan."

It's down to himself and three others. Worm is still not sure if he believes in God or not, figures there's plenty of time to work that out. But in the meantime he prays a lot. It seems to come naturally.

"Brent William Meyer-Hunsberger."

Don't let me be last.

"Voya Innabe Swain.

"Ronald Mark Johnson."

He's last.

9:00 a.m.

Only two other eyes remain in the room, and they're not even looking at Worm. Still, he feels scalded. This whole time Mrs. Truitt has been holding the paper with the names, looking nowhere else, like it's the only thing in the world that matters. He hates Mrs. Truitt. He hates Dead Wednesday. For the last time her mouth opens and her robotic voice speaks:

"Rebecca Ann Finch."

He gets up. As he turns at the head of the aisle, he is surprised to find the teacher looking at him. She seems human again. Something he can't read passes between their eyes.

One black shirt remains on the rack. He grabs it, puts it on. It's way too big. He rolls up the sleeves, does not button it, will *not* be dead. Will *not* play any more of this stupid game than he has to.

Silence . . . closed doors. Alone in the hallway. It's happened before, like going to the boys' room. But he's never gotten the creeps before, never gotten the feeling he's not as alone as he thinks.

9:04 a.m.

And now terror: Worm's throat turns to ice. He's approaching room 101. His first class. Health and Safety. Should he just hang in the hallway? He wants to. He wants to do anything but open the door and become the instant target of a roomful of eyes.

He knows what Eddie would do. Eddie would stroll up and down the hallways and stairwells, a free man. Maybe pop his head into a class or two.

But Eddie is bold. Worm is not.

He stands before the frosted glass and the number 101. The terror is digesting him when his left hand decides on its own to reach out and knock on the door. He wants to kill the hand.

The door opens. It's the teacher, Ms. O'Neill. She leans

56

over his shoulder, looks up and down the hallway, retreats a step, and closes the door in his face.

He stares at the frosted glass. What should he do? Knock again? Just walk in? It's not easy getting the hang of being dead.

Suddenly the door opens again. . . .

Surprise! It's not Ms. O'Neill. It's Claire Meeson the Meek. She's now wearing her black shirt. Gone is the goofy face that yelled "Hip! Hip! Hooray!" in the homeroom doorway. She is somber. She is soft. She lays her hand on his arm and says, not in a whisper, "Come in, Worm."

OK for one Deader to talk to another, Worm figures. Still, she's brave.

He follows her into the room—and can hardly see. The lights are off and the window shades are down. He can barely make out the row of kids on the far side of the room.

He navigates to his usual desk. The door opens and closes. Ms. O'Neill has left the room. But nobody takes advantage. Nobody acts up. Not a whisper. The black shirts darken the darkness.

It's creepy. Worm thinks: *World's biggest coffin.* Thinks:

Score one for the school district. Enough of this and he really might think twice about drinking at sixteen. (Not that he plans to anyway.)

Something is happening up front, at the blackboard. The room's night has puddled in the form of a human. Tall. Boy? Girl? He can't tell. He can hear chalk moving across the board. Apparently finished, the form chucks the chalk into a window shade but does not return to a desk. It crosses the front of the room. The door opens and closes. In that moment of light, Worm thinks he sees something that makes no sense: raspberry-colored pajamas.

The bell rings.

Yelps. Whistles. The door's flung open to a hallway in riot. Dead for forty-four minutes, the class storms out.

Worm turns on the light. There are two enormous words on the blackboard, each letter reaching top to bottom:

DEAD SUCKS

But what gets his attention even more is not so much the dark chalker and the words on the blackboard, but the fact that nobody else seemed to notice.

The hallways are nutso.

Worm remembers this from the previous two years, but now he's the one with the black shirt. He feels he should step into his role, do something wild, but he knows it's not in him. He hopes no one will notice he's acting normally.

Some Deaders are lurching pigeon-toed down the hallway like zombies. So are some of the bolder sixth and seventh graders. He feels a poke in the back, now another. Little runt underclassmen are poking Deaders and chirping things like "RIP, dead meat!" and "Get back in your coffin!" All year long the underclassmen have been grass under the eighth graders' lawn mower. Now the grass is getting its revenge.

Not that the Deaders care. They're too busy having fun, getting the most out of this incredible gift from the town and school district of Amber Springs.

Frisbees are flying. A girl's shoe has become a football. Black shirts are drumming on lockers, moose calls and farts trumpet a snappy rhythm: it's a concert!

Worm pauses at a water fountain. He practically chokes on his mouthful because he gets hip-checked out of the way. "Move it, sonny." A girl's voice, but he doesn't know whose. She's gone in a flash of pajamas. Raspberry. He moves on.

And now a booming voice that rattles the hallway: "KNOCK IT OFF!"

Frisbees clatter to the floor. The rest is silence. It's Mr. Haliburton, the principal. He's new this year.

"PEOPLE DIED! SHOW SOME RESPECT!"

Everyone is frozen. Even upstairs, footsteps stop.

"Fun's over! Get to class!"

Movement in the halls resumes.

Well . . . poop. One growl from the new boss and the good times are over. Worm isn't sure how he feels about that. Even though he was never a participant, it's been fun to watch.

At the bottom of the stairwell Worm meets Eddie, as always, and together they head up to Science. At the turn Eddie stops. He whips out his Wrapper card and shows Worm. It's a gorgeous girl. Long black hair. Her in-quotes name is Kat. Worm looks up to find Eddie grinning at him. He's proud. "Well?" says Eddie.

Worm isn't sure what Eddie is getting at. He shops

61

around for something neutral, safe. He nods, pretends to study the card some more. "Yeah . . . yeah . . . OK."

Eddie thumps him. "O-*kay?*" He snatches the card, points at the picture. "Hottest Wrapper ever, that's all." He holds it in front of Worm's eyes for another look.

Worm knows now what's expected. He puts on his girl-evaluation face, nods. "Yeah," he says firmly. "Totally."

Satisfied, Eddie returns his card to the pocket of his black shirt—and whips out Worm's. Worm knows instinctively this is a game he does not want to play. Thankfully, Eddie only glances at the card and hands it back with a dismissive sniff: "Not impressed."

They resume their climb to the second floor, and every step lifts Worm closer to what may become the most fateful forty-four minutes of his life. One of his classmates in Science will be Beautiful Bijou Newton.

Worm has no experience with this sort of thing. It happened so fast on the bus, he had no time to process it, much less react. What should he do if she targets him again? Fire a smile back? Sure. But what else? Say something? If so, what? What do you do when the most beautiful girl in school singles you out among all others? What would Eddie do? What *will* Eddie do if she announces to the school, *I love Worm?*

62

The last class had no light. This class, Science, has no seats.

They've all been pushed back around the edges. The teacher directs the students to sit on the floor in a circle. When everyone is seated, she comes to the center of the circle and turns a lunch-size paper bag upside down. When she pulls up the bag, a pile of dirt is left on the floor. The teacher crumples the bag and leaves the room.

The circle. The dirt. Such common, familiar things. But here, where they don't belong—they have an effect Worm cannot put a word to.

Twenty-two black shirts in a circle. No one looks up. No one speaks. Twenty of them on their cells. When they glance up from their cells, it's usually at the pile of dirt.

They should have taken everybody's cell. Now *that* would be dead.

Worm's place in the circle is where anyone else would call perfect. He's directly across from Bijou. (A line between them would be the circle's diameter. Halve it for the radius. Area of circle = πr^2.)

He's both thrilled and terrified. He pretends to be busy with his cell phone. Bijou is intently pecking out a text to someone. *OMG—what if it comes up on my screen!* So far it hasn't. Like most of the others, she sits cross-legged. The top she wears is mint green. He dares not stare long and hard enough to be sure, but he thinks there's a similar color on her eyelids.

No instruction to keep quiet has been given or is needed. But things need to be said.

The urge to utter her name is overpowering. Worm whispers to Eddie: "So why did Bijou dump the Hulk?"

Eddie shrugs. "Who knows."

"You think she got tired of him?"

Shrug. "Who knows."

"How did she dump him? Bijou."

"Who knows."

"Maybe she wants somebody in her own grade."

Shrug, no words. He gets a disapproving glare or two, but he can't stop.

"Or maybe she wants to play the field, huh? Bijou?"

"Could be."

Eddie's lack of interest surprises Worm. "Think she has her eye on anybody?"

Shrug.

"Somebody's gonna be a lucky dude."

Not even a shrug.

Worm has used up his first batch of questions. While he's thinking about more Bijou things to say, he steals glances at her. She's now whispering to her neighbor, Mean Monica. Hopefully, she's giving her a few tips on how to be nice. Bijou's honey-blond hair is in a ponytail today. Whispering seems to animate her, as the ponytail swings back and forth. Worm has never seen anything so captivating.

Worm decides he better not be too obvious, so he chats Eddie up about other stuff for a while. And finally circles back: "She doesn't even act like she's beautiful, know what I mean?"

"Who?" says Eddie, who Worm is diverting from his own phone duties.

"Bijou."

Eddie nods.

"And y'know, she's really nice." And figures he better add: "From what I hear."

Shrug.

Interesting how their roles have reversed in this circle around the dirt. Worm the talker, Eddie listening. But of course cool as ever. Worm keeps checking his cell screen for a text, just in case. And he brazenly stares at Bijou for seconds at a time. If she's going to look up and toss him a smile, he doesn't want to miss it. As it turns out, somebody does smile—Mean Monica—so briefly he almost misses it. He wonders who it's aimed at.

Worm is halfway through the next question—"And you know what else"—when Eddie abruptly speaks: "I'm making my move."

Worm is bushwhacked. "Huh? What?"

"Before school lets out."

"Huh?"

"The bus."

Something below Worm's stomach falls off a shelf. "What bus?"

"When she got on. Gave me a dy-no-mite smile."

Worm is standing on a chair with the rope around his neck. Only he can kick the chair away. At last he does. "Who?" he croaks.

The bell rings. Eddie gets up. "Who do you think? The Beautiful One."

10:20 a.m.

Worm finds himself in Social Studies. He doesn't remember walking here. This is another dark room. It fits.

Everything makes sense now. She was smiling at Eddie, not him. *Duh.* Like, really? It's almost funny, now that he thinks of it.

It's been a lunch line of feelings. First he tasted devastation. But to his surprise, devastation came as a tiny portion, just a spoonful on his tray and on to the next feeling, a whole buffet of them. Many he cannot identify. He thinks one might have been envy. Another: brotherhood (with the Hulk). He takes a taste of each and moves on. The only one that isn't small is the last, a big plop in its own bowl. It's relief.

Oh, not that it wasn't wonderful while it lasted. That sweet Cupid's arrow in his chest did things to him that

Eddie could never. Someday, he thinks, if he can work up the nerve, he should thank Bijou. According to his calculations, for 113 minutes he had forgotten about his face.

Confidence. For 113 minutes it was more than a word. For 113 minutes he was admitted to the world of Eddies and Bijous, where the spotlight is a sun that never sets, where bold people never fear looking into a mirror and know exactly what to do with a smile.

But confidence came with a downside. He discovered he was uncomfortable in Eddieworld. Eddie has answers; all Worm has are questions. Eddie's words—"I'm making my move"—sent him back to his comfort zone, back to himself, underground, sliding unseen through the roots of life. Take away the half day of weirdness and freedom, and what's left is a comfortable, familiar fact: for a worm every day is Dead Wednesday.

11:00 a.m.

In Language Arts, Worm decompresses from the early-morning drama. As a sideline watcher, he relies on things happening to him to energize his life. Often the happenings are supplied by Eddie, but Eddie is not in this class. So when his pocket goes *ping* for the hundredth time, Worm decides to give his mom a break. He reads her text:

SHE'S HERE!!!!!!

He pockets the cell. *Tell her to come to the fight,* he think-answers. He looks at the clock. Ninety minutes till fight time. He wonders what Eddie has in mind for the rest of the day.

The desks have all been arranged in pairs—*facing each*

other. Close. The Language Arts teacher, Mr. Fitzpatrick, might as well have written on the blackboard:

WELCOME TO HELL
FOR SHY PEOPLE

And so he finds himself knees to knees with Preston Dodds. Preston arrived in these parts only this year and still knows practically nobody. Like Worm and Claire Meeson, Preston Dodds is shy, and so much less. At least Worm and Claire speak when spoken to and hang with friends. Preston Dodds has been here since September, and in all that time no one has ever detected a personality. He apparently was born without one. Not only does he not speak—he doesn't smile, laugh, clap, cheer, or blow his nose. He's never been seen in the boys' room. He sits in the same seat on the bus every day, cinches his seat belt immediately, and speaks to no one. Whenever possible, he keeps his hands in his pockets, as he is doing now, sitting across from Worm.

Worm looks around. There's almost no eye contact. Kids are looking at their cells or, more than in the other classes, reading a book. Well, it *is* Language Arts.

Nearby, Claire Meeson is knees-up with Monica Biddle. They're whispering, but Worm can hear.

Claire: "I don't know *why* I did it."

Monica: "It wasn't you."

Claire: "It wasn't me."

Worm doesn't have to be a genius to know what they're talking about: Claire at the homeroom doorway, going, "Hip! Hip! Hooray!" He agrees, it wasn't her. And wishes she wouldn't beat herself up over it. She just got caught up in the fun, that's all, before the weird classrooms and Mr. Haliburton yelling, "Show some respect!"

It surprises Worm to see Meeson the Meek being chummy with somebody as prickly as Monica Biddle. It surprises him even more to realize that he hardly ever sees Mean Monica alone.

But he can't listen to whispers and glance around the room forever. Sooner or later his attention is driven to the body smack in front of him, which he's sure is the point of this whole thing. Force them to face each other as flesh-and-blood people, not texts on a screen (as adults are always reminding them), appreciate each other as living creatures so they'll be careful not to kill each other when they get on the road or whatever.

Preston Dodds rarely looks anyone in the eye, or any other part of the face, for that matter. Since he sat down, he's been staring at the bare desktop. It's the only known virtue of Preston Dodds: you can stare at him all you want and he won't look back. He seems to have no cell phone. By comparison, Worm is a circus clown.

Still, shy is shy, which is all it takes for others to ID the two of them as a pair, a perverse brotherhood. As he stares

71

for a moment at the Kid Who Never Looks Back, Worm gets the unsettling feeling that this may be the way others perceive him. Worm Tarnauer = Preston Dodds. Unsettling quickly becomes unbearable.

He looks at the clock. . . .

11:30 a.m.

Sixty minutes till fight time . . . thirteen more min- utes of being in the same lifeless coffin with Preston Dodds.

Which is what drives Worm to do the unthinkable: he stands. Of course, doing so causes every head in class to turn his way, but even that is better than having to face the Kid with No Personality for another second.

He goes to the back of the room, to a place he's never been: Mr. Fitzpatrick's own book collection. Shelves and shelves of books. You can sign one out. Return it late and your fine is the teacher's favorite food, a Reese's peanut butter cup.

He's an alien in Bookland. Books mean two things to Worm: (1) get ready for a test, and (2) clean the cabins of the people who write them.

He has no idea what to look for, can't recall a single title. *Graphic novel,* he thinks. Pictures, at least.

He crouches, tilts his head to title-read, and . . . "Doink."

That same voice . . . the water fountain girl's . . . and something hitting his ear. A little green nugget plipping to the floor. And here's the voice again, friendly this time— "Tic Tac?"—and a hand is coming into his field of vision, and sure enough, it's holding a tiny, clear plastic box of more little green nuggets. "Hold out your hand," the voice says. He holds out his hand, and the tiny box shakes and three Tic Tacs drop into his palm. "Put them in your mouth. Never know when somebody'll wanna kiss you." The voice is more than just friendly, as if it knows him. But he can't place it. He puts the mints in his mouth. His eyes follow the arm—raspberry pj sleeve—up to the shoulder and on to the smile . . . the face. . . .

11:32 a.m.

"Worm . . . *Worm!* . . ."

The voice is distant, like it's coming from the far end of a tunnel.

"Worm . . . wake up."

Faces . . . faces swimming above him . . .

"He's choking!"

Pounding on his back . . . A sound comes out of his mouth, followed by three little green nuggets, falling to the floor, rolling. . . . What's he doing on the floor at the back of the room?

Faces swimming . . . Claire Meeson . . . Monica Biddle . . . Otter, others, crowding, worried . . .

He stares at the little green nuggets . . . remembers something . . . Tic Tacs . . . *face.* . . .

Hands lug him, prop him against the bookshelves . . . voices pepper:

"What happened?"

"You OK?"

"He fainted."

"Did he eat breakfast?"

"Did you eat breakfast?"

"Help him up."

"No, let him sit. Don't move him."

"He just *fainted*, moron. He didn't get hit by a truck."

"Can you stand, Worm?"

He's tired. He thinks he just wants to sit here for a while.

"I'm getting the nurse." Claire Meeson's voice.

"No!" he shouts, the prospect of attention knocking him back to himself.

He gropes for a shelf. Hands pull him to his feet.

"What happened, Worm?"

Give them an answer. End this. "Skipped breakfast," he lies through the grog. "Desk."

Hands help him, wobbling, to his desk. Hands, voices fussing over him. A hand in his face holds the three green Tic Tacs.

"Who were you expecting to kiss, Worm?" It's Otter.

Big yuks all around. Relief too, he can tell.

"I know what happened," says Mean Monica, grinning

in his face. "He wandered too close to the books and got dizzy and fainted!"

Louder yuks this time. Worm's allergy to books is well known.

He waves them away, prays for the bell to ring. "I'm good," he tells them. "Never skip breakfast."

They drift back to their seats. They try not to stare. They're as intent as he is to pretend nothing happened. Nobody is paying the least bit of attention to the girl in pajamas sitting on his desk.

"Oh boy. I was afraid of this. You OK now?"

It's her. The "doink" voice. The sitter on his desk. The brain burp that happened at the bookshelves has followed him to his seat. Inches away, Mr. Personality stares at his desktop.

Unlike many of his teenage classmates, Worm hasn't yet left the days of obedience behind. He follows the rules. Somebody tells him to do something, he does it. Ask him a question, he answers.

He nods.

Huge release of minty breath above him. "Great." A hand squeezes his shoulder.

"You can look, Worm," the voice says. "I won't bite."

It's come to this. Deep inside he knows now. But doesn't

know. Believes. But doesn't believe. Can. Not. Believe. But the voice knows him . . . knows his name. . . .

The hand is still on his shoulder. He looks. Resists the temptation to touch it. Follows it up the arm to the shoulder, the neck, the face . . . which hasn't changed. It's the face from the back of the room.

The face on the card.

The poster.

The face of Rebecca Ann Finch.

She smiles, giggles. "I was going to try a dumb joke, like, 'You look like you saw a ghost.' But I won't. Know why?"

"Why?" he says, not thinking.

Several heads in the class turn. *Be careful.*

"Because you don't look that way."

She's right. Baffled? Unhinged? Out of his gourd? Yes. But scared? No.

She's holding out the little plastic box. "Tic Tac? Try again?"

He just stares. So she pours several into her own hand and pops them into her mouth, closes her eyes, rattles them around, going, "Mmm . . . mmm." Now her face is sideways into his. She opens her mouth, showing her green tongue, and he gets a minty gust as she goes "Huhhh . . ." into his face. "Am I kissable now?"

He nods dumbly.

"Where's the card?" she says, still friendly but businessy now too. "Hah . . . ," she goes, "where else?" She reaches into his pocket, pulls out the card. She groans. "I have *never* taken a good picture in my *life.*" She punches his shoulder, hard, like it's his fault.

Twenty-five faces turn. Claire Meeson is rising, pointing. "*You* . . . are going to the nurse."

He plucks the card from Becca's hand, shoves it in his pocket (only later will he wonder: *What did* they *see?*), stands. "Going. Nurse," he blurts as he runs from the room, leaving a wake of black shirts and mouths in the shape of eggs.

11:39 a.m.

In the hallway.

Worm walks. Stops. Tries to sense if he's alone. Not sure. Takes a deep breath, turns around. She's not there.

Maybe it was just a classroom thing. The Dead Wed Effect. Probably hit his head when he fainted. He feels for a bump.

Boys' room. He heads there.

11:40 a.m.

Worm busts in. Hunches in front of the stalls, hands on knees, gasping, like he's just finished a marathon.

A deep breath.

A glass of water.

Sit down.

Walk.

He's thinking of all the things you're supposed to do when you're stressed out, stuff he's seen on TV.

Count to ten.

Hit a punching bag.

Scream.

"'Sup, dude?"

He jerks up. Two black-shirted Deaders are at the urinals. He didn't notice. With all the free-ranging eighth graders, Dead Wed is the busiest day of the year in the BR.

Worm waves. "No problem. Got a cold. Congested." He fakes a cough.

One of them nods, chuckles. "Didn't want to miss today, huh? Going to the fight too?"

Worm gives a thumbs-up.

Splash water on your face.

He goes to a sink, splashes water on his face . . . cups his hands . . . drinks. . . .

The black shirts are leaving. The talky one sends a guy punch to his shoulder. "You da Deader."

And they're out the door.

"You forgot to wash your hands!"

It's her. Calling after them. She's behind him, in the mirror.

They do *show in mirrors.*

"Go ahead and pee if you want," she says. "I won't look."

The bell rings.

Worm lurches for the door.

"Stop!"

"School's out! I'm out! I'm a Deader!" Eddie! Fight! Freedom!

"Worm! *Please!*"

He stops. He doesn't turn. He won't turn. He won't look at her. It. He won't speak to something that doesn't exist. He hears her approaching footsteps. They stop behind him. Her voice is gentle, kind of motherly in a pleading way. He's pretty sure she's going to touch him, but she doesn't. "Worm, we have to work together on this. I don't know what's going on any more than you. Please, Worm."

Worm turns. He has to look up to see her eyes. Remembers she's seventeen. Was. He's already missed a minute of freedom.

He wants to run.

He wants to stay.

"To tell you the truth," she says, "I'm amazed that you hung in there this long." She squeezes his shoulder. "Thanks, Worm. Really."

Somewhere inside him a warm wave kisses a shore.

"OK," she says with a snap in her voice. "Let's get this outta the way. Do you believe in ghosts?"

"No," he says automatically, and wonders if he's hurt her feelings. She's wearing fluffy, shaggy slippers that match her pj's: raspberry.

Freedom-bound kids are thundering past the BR door.

"Neither do I," she says. "I don't have a clue any more than you do."

"How can you not believe?" he says. "You *are* one. How can you not believe in yourself?"

"I believe in me, not in ghosts."

"So what *are* you?"

Is he really having this conversation?

She shrugs. "Who knows? Does it matter? All I know is one minute there was the tree, and next thing I know, I'm in a bottle."

As if Worm's not already confused enough. "Bottle?"

She waves it away. "I'll tell you later. Hey"—with her finger she traces a circle above her head, flaps her arms like wings—"maybe I'm an angel."

"You're no angel," he says, which sends her laughing, staggering into a stall door.

"Touché," she says.

"So why are you here? Why me? Why aren't you in a graveyard somewhere?"

"Suddenly I was out of the bottle and into your school hallway and there you were, at the water fountain."

"But why me? How'd you know my name?"

"I don't know. I just knew." She laughs. "Hah—duh—and one little thing that made it pretty obvious you were the one."

"What?"

"Nobody else could see me."

"What bottle?" he says.

"Hold your horses. We'll get to that later."

"Later? There's gonna be a *later*?"

She laughs more. Something about him seems to tickle her. "'Fraid so, dude. Like, it's . . . *Dead* Wednesday?" She air-quotes *Dead*. "And *I* want to know why *I'm* here as much as you do."

She snatches her card from his pocket again. She looks at it, wags her head, frowns, suddenly perks up. She holds the card next to her face. "OK, seriously now. Tell me the truth. You won't hurt my feelings. Am I or am I not better-looking than the warthog in this picture?"

He studies them both, face and picture. "Drop the fake camera smile," he says. She drops it. He nods. "You're better."

"In person."

He nods. "In person."

In person?

She looks back at the card, snarls. "Oh, for crying out loud. Do you *believe* this? 'Bottles lightning bugs.'" She throws the card to the floor—"Once!"—stomps on it. "One time I bottled lightning bugs. I was *six*, for God's sake. I woke up the next morning and they were all dead. Because I didn't poke holes in the lid. And *this* is all they can say about me, like it's all my life added up to, like, 'Oh yeah, the Finch girl. The notorious lightning bug bottler. Right up there with Vlad the Impaler.'"

"Who's that?" he says.

"And they are *not* lightning bugs. They are fireflies. Cockroaches are *bugs*. Thousand-leggers are *bugs*." She pokes him in the chest. "The firefly is the official insect of the state of Pennsylvania." Pokes again. "Didn't know *that*, did you, Worminator?"

Playing games with his name, like his father.

She picks up the card, hands it to him. "Sorry. Sometimes I'm impulsive."

Already the hallway is quiet. The Deaders have broken the world record for vamoosing school.

She rolls up her raspberry pajama sleeve. She holds out her arm. "Pinch me."

"Huh?" he says.

"Pinch me. So you know I'm real. Pinch me."

He stares at the arm. Magicians do this: feel this, feel that. Is that what all this is? He's inside a magician's trick?

"Pinch me!"

He pinches her.

She yells: "Owww!" She punches his shoulder. "That *hurt*."

"You *said*," he says.

"I didn't say mutilate me." She rubs the spot. It's red. His thumbnail mark shows. "Satisfied?" she says.

He can't speak, can't think.

She's studying his face. "Shy, huh?"

He says nothing.

Her eyes are true as a mirror, but better. She smiles, nods. "Pimples."

He stiffens. The word sends tremors through him. It's the word that defines him more than any other, yet he cannot bear to hear it, to read it, to even think it. "I had a pimple once," she says. Like, *I had an itch once.* "A monster. Right"—she fingertips a spot on her chin—"here. I know. No comparison."

And now—*what!*—she's patting his cheek . . . and now she's running the tip of her forefinger across the bumps. He jerks back. Even *he* doesn't do that. "Stop!" he screams, his voice resounding in the boys' room.

She leans in; he feels her lips move against his ear as she whispers: "Worm, it's OK. It doesn't matter."

Yeah, sure, he thinks, *One-Pimple Girl. Tell me it's OK when you wake up with a face full of them someday. Tell me when they start taking school pictures of knees and elbows instead of faces.*

It happens too fast for him to react: she leans down and kisses him, right on a bump. Somehow her kiss confirms her reality more than his pinch.

"Where's the auditorium?" she says abruptly.

Thrilled to change the subject, he ushers her into the empty hallway. He points. "That way."

She grabs his hand, pulls him. "C'mon. I never got to do this."

He has to run to keep up.

The auditorium is dark and empty. Becca sprints down the aisle, hand-vaults herself onto the stage. Tamps her hands as if asking for wild applause to stop, standing ovationers to be seated. "Thank you . . . thank you"—facing in turn each quarter of the auditorium—"please . . . thank you . . . thank you . . . you're too kind. . . ." After at least two minutes of this, she drops her arms, shuts up. Suddenly Worm feels like the place really is full and he's the only one left standing. He sits, somewhere in the middle.

"I wrote this," she says in the darkness, like a shadow speaking, "not very long ago."

She begins to sing. She has a good enough voice. OK for a high school choir, he figures. Hits the notes.

He expected something sassy, like her. Maybe hip-hop, rap. But it's not. It starts out happy—he knows this even

90

without understanding much of it—and ends up somewhere else. From what he can tell, it's about two streams pouring into a cup—he thinks one of them might be her—but there's a hole in the bottom of the cup, and when she goes to drink it (can you be the drink *and* the drinker?), nothing's there. The cup is empty. Whatever, it's not the meaning of the words that touches him, but how she sings them, like she's not taking them from the dictionary, but planting them in a beautiful garden. The musical notes are rain.

No big fuss, no thank-yous when she finishes. Apparently, the crowd is either unimpressed or stunned into silence. He discovers he's standing, clapping.

She calls from the stage: "Thank you for crying." He didn't know he was. "I always thought, 'Man, I wish I could write a song that makes people cry.'"

The shadow hops down from the stage, hurries to him. She hugs him. "You *really* liked it?" she says. "You're not just being nice?"

"I liked it," he says. He loved it.

She grabs his hand and hauls him, running, from the auditorium. "Let's blow this dump!"

The school property is empty as a Sunday morning.

"Which way's the action?" Becca says.

Worm's never heard the word *action* paired with Amber Springs.

"Downtown," she says.

It's a half block away. Pocono Street. She marches off, still holding his hand.

Only now is he getting over the embarrassment of crying at her song. He thought he was past all that.

She stops at every storefront on Pocono. Baskerville's Pharmacy . . . Best Man men's shop . . . Jake the barber . . . She's all eyes and squealy comments, like Amber Springs is New York or something.

She hangs so long in front of Fiona's Fashions that his eyes are driven to his watch.

"I gotta go!" Worm wails.

Becca doesn't even turn from the store window. "Really? Where?"

"The fight. Jeep Waterstone and Snake Davis. They're finally gonna settle it. Everybody's gonna be there. Already there." Another glance at his watch. "Fifteen minutes! Even girls. Maybe even teachers! It's the biggest thing of the whole school year! Maybe ever!"

Well, at least that got her to turn around and face him. "Wow," she says, the weakest "wow" he's ever heard. "And where is this biggest thing ever going to happen?"

"At the cannon in the park. Over there." He points. It's a five-minute walk. He'll trot. He can feel his muscles getting twitchy, like he's going to be in the fight. "I gotta get a good spot. The cannon seats are long gone by now."

93

She shakes her head, pretends to be pondering. "Long gone . . . long gone . . ."

She's mocking him. He's had enough of this infuriating, clueless outsider. He turns and heads off, breaks into a trot . . . and is stone-shocked to feel her steely grip on his upper arm, yanking him to a stop. She squares up to him, her face serious now, the mocky twinkle gone from her eyes. "OK, now let me see if I have this straight. If I don't, you're free to go. OK? Deal?" She holds out her hand.

He reluctantly shakes her hand, says nothing. He knows she's out of his league. Makes no difference that the fight is real and she isn't. Can't be.

"OK . . . so . . . ," she begins. "What you're saying is . . . you would rather go see a couple of dumbos slap each other around than be with me"—she thumb-points to herself—"*me* . . . a . . . uh . . ." Her shoulders flump with exasperation. "We gotta find a name for me. 'Ghost' was just a default. Something that's *me.* Any ideas?"

Like she doesn't know his head is empty as a balloon right now. "Well," she says, "I've been giving it some thought. Now tell me how this strikes you . . . *spectral maiden.*"

She's too pleased with herself to conceal it. Like he's really got a choice here. "Sounds good," he manages to say.

She nods perkily, all happy. "It *does,* doesn't it? It's me."

She's looking at him like a dog at dinner. She wants *more.* "Yeah," he says.

"Yeah," she repeats, with a fist pump and a satisfied growl. "So . . . you'd rather go see a fight than spend time with a spectral maiden—in other words, you want to walk away from what is probably the most unique experience in the history of humanity. Did I get any of that wrong?"

He's smart enough to know when he's walked into an answer trap. She's got his head looped like a funnel cake. His only hope is that she'll see his problem and take over the driver's seat . . . which she does. She grabs his hand and pulls him up Pocono. He can feel his skin scraping as he exits the jaws of his dilemma.

His exiting dialogue with his brain:

Dude, the fight's real. She isn't.

Yeah? Tell her *that.*

They're standing in front of the Play It Again Sam thrift shop. A lady in shorts and blue socks comes out. Becca Finch sends her a stage whisper: "Boo." The lady gives Worm a look and heads up the street. "Do they have hats in there?" Becca calls to the lady, who keeps walking.

Becca walks in. Not through the door. She opens it, closes it. Leaves him like a dummy on the sidewalk.

A brilliant idea lands on him like a Boeing 747. He can have it both ways! He can run to the fight, watch the fight, and run back to meet her anywhere she wants, store of her choice. She can have him the rest of the day.

And just as fast, brilliant turns to stupid. He hardly knows her, spectral maiden or whatever, and yet in some sense he can't put his finger on, he knows her well. And one of the things he knows is that, whether he's her assignment or not, not in a million years is she going to play that game. With Becca Finch there's no having it both ways. He enters Play It Again Sam.

For an instant he thinks it's his mother, the person in the back, because she's wearing a floppy gray felt hat, its circular brim wide as a sombrero. His mother wears one like it in the garden. But of course it's not his mother. His mother wouldn't be wearing pajamas. And when she turns, her smile is practically as wide as the hat. She poses flirtily. "Like it?"

"It's OK," he says. As if the hat isn't bad enough, it's got a yellow feather in the band.

She goes into fake shock. "Wow—rave review!" She swoons. "Somebody catch me."

He laughs.

"Pay for it," she says. She hip-checks him and breezes out the door.

He turns to the counter. The lady at the cash register is

so stiff, he thinks at first she's a secondhand mannequin for sale. Then she blinks. He wonders what she saw. A floppy hat floating out the door? He has no idea what a thrift shop hat costs. He dumps his only money—a five—on the counter and hurries out.

She's half a block away, not waiting for him.

Worm has heard of riptides. People at the shore standing in the ocean, maybe only up to their knees, and a riptide grabs them and carries them out to sea. Fighting it is useless. They're never seen again. He catches up to Becca.

If she wasn't already, now with the hat she's the center-piece of the town. Wide and floppy as it is, it looks like a giant manta ray with a yellow feather. "Oh . . . ," she goes, looking surprised. "It's you. I figured you slipped away to the big fight."

She moves toward him in a way he's never seen a girl move before. *Walk* is not the word. She's grinning with in-tentions he can't read. "So . . . ," she says, actually more purrs than says. "This must mean you like me. You must"—she hip-checks him—"wanna dance."

She hip-checks him again, and this time she says "Boop" when their hips bump. And next time his hip meets hers halfway, and they both go, "Boop," and laugh.

And keep doing it: "Boop . . . boop . . . boop . . ." In between "boops" she wiggles her hips, shakes her shoulders. And—*riptide*—so does he. Right there in the sun, the mother of all spotlights, on the sidewalk in downtown Amber Springs, PA. Shy Worm Tarnauer. They laugh and continue on up the street, and it occurs to him that he has just danced for the first time in his life—with a girl, no less.

"Mommy, Mommy, look! A Deader!"

It's a little kid with a mother, him in one hand and a canvas tote bag big enough to hold the kid in the other. At first he thinks the kid is referring to Becca, then remembers the black shirt he's wearing. He should have ditched it.

"Don't look," says the mother. "We don't see him." She pulls the kid into creaky-floored Dollar General.

Him. Not *them.*

He wonders if he's special, can see dead people—dance with them—like the kid in *Sixth Sense.* Special. Take that, Mean Monica.

She's turned away from him, her snappy self gone. He suddenly senses she may not be here all day. Whatever is going on, he hasn't gotten the hang of it yet.

"So . . . how big's the bottle?" he says, anything to get her back in the game.

She sniffs. "Big," she says. She turns. Her eyes are red. She points to the steeple of the Presbyterian church. "Like that high."

"Wow," he says, meaning it. It's goofy, but he's feeling fatherly toward this tall, older girl. "*That's* a big-ass bottle."

She can't help it—a gaspy laugh comes out, and suddenly she's smothering him in a hug. She's a hugger, like his dad.

"It was only once," he says, muffled, into her neck, thinking of the fireflies.

He feels her nodding above him, feels her swell and deflate with a deep breath. "I know . . . I know. . . ." She lets him go, starts pacing randomly about the sidewalk. "It's . . ." She stares at him, still finding nothing in his face. "There's no time in there, Worm. Y'know?" Worm nods. Like, sure, he knows. "It's always, like, now, this instant." She snaps her fingers. "But at the same time it's a trillion trillion this instants, a *now* that never ends."

"So . . . ," he says, working on it, trying to put it together, "you weren't kidding."

She blinks. "What?"

"The blackboard. 'DEAD SUCKS.' "

"Hah." She gives a snorty laugh that's not a laugh. She paces, paces. "Yeah . . . what's the date?"

Seven days and a wake-up. "June ninth," he says.

She's counting on her fingers. "December twenty-fourth. Almost six months . . ." More counting. "Was February twenty-eight days this year?"

"Yes." This was not a leap year.

"How many days in April?"

"Thirty." He's liking this. He wishes she would ask him the number of days in every month. He knows them all.

"May?"

"Thirty-one."

Counting: ". . . one forty-nine, one fifty . . ." She looks at him like she's in water floundering and he's the only one on deck with a life preserver. "Oh . . . my . . . God . . . ," she says, wondrous, disbelieving. "One hundred and sixty-seven days, Worm. Your days. That's how long I was in the bottle."

And suddenly a life preserver is in his hands. He flings it to her. "But you're *out*. You're here now."

And she's hugging him again. "Sweet Worm . . ."

She seems in no hurry to let go. He's not complaining. He wonders, when you're alone with them, if all girls are this emotional.

In time, over her shoulder, he sees the door of Dollar General opening. . . .

12:29 p.m.

And out comes the shopping lady with her kid, tote bag bulging.

Right away the kid spots Worm and yaps, "Deader!"

"Stop it," his mother snaps, and yanks him up the street. The kid is pulling at her hand like a puppy on a leash. What does he think he's going to do if she lets go? Run over and bite him?

Somehow, the kid manages to break free, but to Worm's surprise, the kid doesn't come charging at him. What he does is repeat with a sneer—"Deader!"—and now he's turning around and bending over and aiming a fart at Worm that's loud and rumble-deep enough to have come from a sumo wrestler . . . and Becca has suddenly dropped from his arms and is now on the sidewalk. Her knees are drawn up and her fists are pounding the pavement, and Worm is wondering if it's dangerous to laugh so hard.

When she's finally finished, she grabs his black shirt and pulls herself to her feet and wags her head and gasps. "Whew . . . ," she goes. "I needed that."

He's never seen somebody laugh and cry in such a short period of time.

She takes his hand, pulls. "C'mon. I want to walk. I want to walk forever."

Hand in hand they go down Pocono Street, past Crafts R Us . . . Jo-Anne Doughnuts . . . Zummo Hardware. . . . He's thinking he hasn't held a girl's hand since first or second grade, students following teachers like baby ducks. He can't figure out if she's being motherly, girlfriendy, or something else. She's looking this way and that, stops to peek in windows, says a friendly "Hi!" to unresponsive sidewalkers.

At last she gives his hand a quick squeeze: she's returning her attention to him. "So, yeah, I'm out. I'm here. Question is, for how long? Question is, why?" She looks at him. "We know the who."

"We do?" he says.

"Oh yeah."

"Who?"

"You."

"Why me?" he says.

"Bingo," she says. "That's the question. It's kinda fuzzy. Like, I *know* it's you. I knew it when I saw you at the water fountain." She sandwiches his face between her hands. "I'm here for you, Robbie Tarnauer. You need me."

"I do?" And thinks: *I could list forty kids right now who need changing more than me.*

She nods firmly. "Yeah. You do."

They walk a ways in silence. Worm ponders. Pondering is nothing new to Worm. He often tunes in to the birthplace of his own words, sees them percolate up to his mind, into his mouth, where, more often than not, they stay. He seldom lets them out.

They're passing the First United Methodist church. They're not holding hands anymore.

"I need to know what makes you tick, Worm."

He doesn't like the sound of that, doesn't want to be investigated.

"It's not pimples," she states flatly. "I won't *let* it be."

"What pimples?" he says, and she's cracking up before the words dry out.

She pokes him in the chest. "There's more than shy in there, kid. There's funny." She studies him. "I bet before you got shy, you were a performer."

I'm a Little Teapot.

She takes his hand again, swinging it as they stroll along Pocono Street for all the world to see. One minute he feels like her kid, her being taller and older and ordering him around and all. The next minute he feels like they're boyfriend and girlfriend . . . hah, yeah, like *he* would know what having a girlfriend feels like.

They're passing Mike's. WORLD'S BEST HOAGIES. Closest thing in town to a kids' hangout. Eddie chills here. So would Worm if he lived in town.

"So, Worm," she says, shoulder-nudging him as they pass the Apple Walnut Café, "c'mon, spill it, what can I do for you? What do you *need*?"

Worm's brain is a blank. He's got Eddie. He's got *Nuke 'Em ALL Now!* Endless, schoolless summer awaits. Seven days and a wake-up. What else is there? Life is good. "I'm OK," he says.

She's wagging her head. "Sorry, Worm. You're not getting off that easy. So let's see. . . ." She raises his hand over his head and twirls him around like he's the girl in a dance—it's embarrassing, but something else too. "Let's start easy. What's your favorite color?"

"Red," he says. It's not. He just says it to keep her happy. He's known for years he's supposed to have a favorite color, but so far he hasn't been able to decide. Maybe that will come along with maturity too.

"Hmm," she goes, squinting at him sideways under the slouchy hat brim that halves the distance between them; she knows he's lying. "How original. OK . . . best friend?"

"Eddie Fusco."

"Favorite food?"

"Oyster stew."

It just came out. That's how he knows it's true. Ever since he saw his father eating it at the Gateway Diner. He couldn't have been more than five or six.

"Ugh," she goes, making a face. "Kids don't like oysters. They're slimy."

"Sorry," he says.

"Favorite sport."

"Ping-Pong."

Another squint. He knows he's supposed to say football or whatever, but he saw Ping-Pongers on TV in the Olympics once, and he could not believe how they did it. Because he's tried at Uncle Bill's. He'd say football if it was Eddie asking.

"Favorite song."

He's stumped. He's not into music yet like a lot of his classmates. Another race he's trailing in. He remembers "Onward, Christian Soldiers" from Sunday school, but he's pretty sure that doesn't count. Or Christmas carols. At Eddie's house once he heard a song called "Yellow Submarine." He still wonders what it means. Well, *yellow submarine*, of course, but what the hell does *that* mean? Whatever, he woke up for days with the tune in his head. "'Yellow Submarine,'" he says.

She laughs. He doesn't remember ever making some-body laugh so much. He knows he's her assignment, but he can't help feeling there's something more personal going on here too. He wishes he could compare notes with Eddie. . . .

Eddie!

He looks at his watch. . . .

"It's over!" Worm wails. He *still* can't let it go.

Becca looks at his watch, nods sympathetically. "Ah. Y'think it's over by now? Eleven minutes? *If* it started on time?"

"You kidding?" he says (not that he's a boxing expert or anything). "Eleven minutes? You can't slug it out for eleven minutes. It was probably over in eleven *seconds*." He pictures a roundhouse right—or maybe an uppercut, lifting one or the other clear off his feet . . . Jeep . . . Snake . . . one of them on the ground, flat like a snow angel . . . glazed eyes staring at nothing . . . the crowd going wild, the cannon rocking.

She drapes a consoling arm over his shoulders. "Sorry, Worm. I know it meant a lot to you. Hey . . ." She backs off, chipper, challenging. "C'mon, you wanna duke?" She's dancing on her toes, like Muhammad Ali in films he's seen.

She's flicking jabs that land an inch from his nose, quacking at him: "Let's go, big boy. Put 'em up. Scared of a girl, huh? Scared somebody will see you getting beat up by a girl?" Jab, jab. "Pow! Pow!" One of them actually nips the end of his nose.

Worm, like many boys, grew up believing any boy can beat up any girl. Difference in size means nothing. It's nature. Boys are stronger and faster and that's that. Eddie himself has said he could beat up his mother with one hand behind his back if he *wanted* to, and his mother is five nine.

Now, with this girl, this spectral maiden, sparring in front of him, snarling even . . . well, he knows she's just kidding, but he also knows something else: if he seriously tried to hit her, he would find himself seriously decked on the sidewalk.

She's dropped her gloves now but is still dancing, feinting left and right. And into his head comes the dialogue on the bus tomorrow, maybe the worst thing of all:

Eddie: *Hey, man, where were you?*

Worm: *Oh yeah . . . right . . . well, y'know, listen, Ed . . . I know this sounds, like, goofy* [finger-quote "goofy"], *but listen, I met this dead chick—y'know, the one on my card?—and so we decided to go strolling up Pocono Street instead. By the way, who won?*

If only because it's the *only* thing he can think of to *do*, he looks at his watch.

Worm and a dork named Albert are the only eighth graders who wear a watch to school. He knows he can tell the time on his cell, but he likes the look of the minute and hour hands. For some reason his watch makes him think of his father in the army. But mostly it's kind of a compass that positions him in time and space. One glance at his wrist and he always knows where he fits. Who he is.

Except this time.

He turns from Becca, from everything, and walks up Pocono . . . walks up Pocono. . . .

No one is stopping him, no hand yanking him to a halt. He wanted a free day, he got it. The sun's glare off the shadowless sidewalk is blinding.

Is she behind him? Has she gone off the other way, given up on him? The farther he walks, the more he's tempted to

110

turn around. He fights it. He's passing Mean Monica's bus stop.

He's passing downtown's last store, Lamp Repair & More, when she goes prancing past him. And that's it: *prancing.* Part run, part dance, all Finch.

Somewhere along the line he expects she will stop, turn, laugh, and wait for him. She doesn't.

She's the size of a fingernail now. She's at the edge of town, nearing Forrest, passing Jimmy's Auto Repair.

He walks. He refuses to run. He will *not* run after her. (OK, he walks a little fast.)

As he draws nearer, he is struck by how much she seems to be enjoying herself, lah-dee-dahing along, stopping like a dog to sniff out every little thing, making him stop-start, stop-start. He can't see her face, but he knows she is smiling big-time. Every so often she pops a Tic Tac into her mouth. He's only a few steps behind her now—he can hear her humming—but he likes this, discovers maybe he doesn't want to totally catch up. It bothers him for a moment to think that she's not missing him, seems perfectly happy without him, maybe doesn't even know he's right behind her. She stops. He stops. She picks a black-eyed Susan from a front yard and flips it back over her shoulder. He catches it. She waltzes on. Her fluffy raspberry slippers *shsh-shsh* on the pavement. He thinks: *Dying surprised her.* Sadness soaks him.

She speaks: "Are we heading the right way?"

"For what?" he says.

"Your house. I want to see where you live. Meet your parents. Figure this out."

"I don't live in a house," he says.

"Really?" she says. "So . . . what? A cave? Tepee?"

"Well, yeah, it's a *house* house, but it's a lot more. It's a retreat kinda place. For writers. They stay in cabins."

She stops, turns. "Seriously?"

He nods. He can't believe how good it is to see her face again.

She resumes walking. "So are we going the right way?"

"Yeah," he says. "But it's too far to walk."

"How far?"

"Five, six miles."

She stops. She takes off her fluffies, walks on, picking up the pace, fluffies in hand. She doesn't wear nail polish, toes or fingers.

"Why are you wearing slippers?" he says. "And pajamas?"

She stops, so abruptly he almost plows into her. She looks up, gives a deep sigh. She's breathing hard. "Pooter," she says, and resumes walking.

He senses it's time to keep his trap shut. He knows she's supposed to be interrogating him, not the other way around. He thinks he wants to be alongside her now, but he's afraid to change anything.

She speaks: "I say that—I tell *myself* that. But I know better. *He* didn't put me in that bottle."

She sniffs. She stops. This time Worm knows: she's waiting for him.

He's alongside her now, arms touching. He has a goofy thought—she seems to trigger goofy thoughts—of putting his arm around her, sticking his hand under that hat and tousling her hair and saying something like, *It's OK, kid. Tell me about it.*

But it's she who makes the move. She leans her head to the side until it's resting on Worm's shoulder—tricky because his shoulder is lower than hers and because they're still walking. Eddie's words—"I'm making my move"—come back to him, but suddenly they don't feel so intimidating. He wonders if someday he'll have a move of his own. He wonders if even now it's developing somewhere inside him, maturing.

When Becca straightens up, she slides her left arm under his right, like women do with men, and tells him the story.

"It was a little thing," Becca says. **"That's the most** important. Say it, Worm, so I'll know you know."

"It was a little thing."

The sun is high. The shadow line of the hat brim runs under her nose from ear to ear, leaving only her mouth in sunlight, giving the impression that it's not so much a part of her as *representing* her, speaking *for* her.

It was all about Pooter.

Pooter was her boyfriend. His real name was Harmon Dean Baker.

It was December 23, the last day of school before Christmas vacation. But the groundwork was laid long before that.

"He was beautiful," she says. "Even pretty girls were jealous. He was everything. Class president. Star jock. Sings!

114

Played Seymour in *Little Shop of Horrors*. Smart. And *nice*! What's not to like? He was the perfect human being." She looks at Worm. "Understand?"

He nods. Thinking: *Eddie*. Thinking: *Maybe every school has one*.

She stops, steps back, takes off her hat, spreads her arms. "Now look at me. How would you rate me, one to ten?"

Inexperienced as he is, Worm in his role as observer considers himself a competent judge. He takes the question seriously, frankly looks her over. She's by no means Bijou beautiful. Prom court? No. Cheerleader? Maybe. "Nine," he lies.

She laughs. She plunks the hat on his head and kisses his nose. "You're a really bad liar, Worm. But you're sweet."

They resume walking. Worm appreciates the shade too much to object to the hat. The sun is super bright today.

"So . . . ," she says, "you can see why I was knocked for a loop when one day he's coming out of Waldo's—the local pizza hangout—just as I'm going in, and he holds the door for me and sort of bows and says, 'Milady,' and I play my part and I curtsy and say, 'Thank you, good sir,' and I figure that's that. Except I take two steps inside and discover that he's right behind me. Now I'm confused. 'I thought you were leaving,' I say. 'So did I,' he says.

"Well, I'm so dumb I'm thinking, 'I guess he forgot something. Whatever.' But the thing is, I can't move. He's got

115

this look on his face I can't read. It's not a grin, it's not a smile. Whatever it is, it's keeping me stuck there like there's superglue on my soles. And he's sure not looking around for something he forgot. He's looking at me. I mean *me*. Like I'd never been looked at. And the only thing my brain can come up with is, 'Uh-oh, girl,' and I'm praying he says something, because no way can I produce language.

"And then he says, 'I'm getting tomato pie with anchovies. What about you?'

"Which is totally bogus because he already ate, which I know because he's still got the napkin tucked into his pants, the klutz—yeah, he's adorable too. I think I said something brilliant, like, 'Uh,' and next thing I know, he's bowing again and sweeping his arm forward and leading me to a booth.

"It all gets pretty dazy after that. Like, what's really happening? Is there a girl in another booth that he's trying to make jealous? I don't remember what I ordered. I do remember sneaking a look around and finding no girl in another booth. I remember a thought that made no sense and yet kept repeating itself over and over: 'Harmon Dean Baker is having two lunches because of me.'

"We talked. I don't remember what about, but I know we talked nonstop. That was the first thing, and it never changed. We were great talkers with each other. We were still talking when we left Waldo's. He walked me home . . . talked me home. Then we talked over to his house. Then

116

we talked to the park and around town and went back to Waldo's and talked through dinner and walked and talked some more until it was dark. We knew we were being ridiculous—we kept saying so—but it was like we were on a train that wouldn't slow down enough for us to hop off. When he walked me home for the second time, the stars were out, and he said, 'We gotta stop this,' and I said, 'Stop what?' and he said, 'Stop talking. We need duct tape. Tape our mouths shut,' and before I had a chance to laugh, he was kissing me and I was kissing back, and when I came to and opened my eyes, I thought the stars had come down— but it was fireflies, dancing and winking around us. This was a Saturday in August. August fifteenth."

Worm may be still waiting for his social maturity to catch up with his underarm hair, but he knows a great love story when he hears one. He likes how she's taken his arm, like they're man and wife in an old black-and-white movie. He keeps his elbow out, like he's supposed to. He wishes he didn't know the ending isn't happy.

She pulls him close, grins. "You wish it would end there, don't you?"

He can't speak. He nods.

She squeezes him closer, leans in for a head touch. "Me too," she says. "But hey"—another quick change, back to cheery—"I counted the days. A hundred and thirty-two. Total. And a hundred and thirty-one were heaven. How many people can say that?" She sighs. She looks at the sky, mouth wide open, as if inviting it in. "I'll tell you, Worm, dead does wonders for your optimism. I look back and the glass is always half-full." She smiles, closes her eyes, wags her head. "The times we had."

She says nothing for a while. Thinking about those times, Worm figures. He doesn't dare disturb her. They walk . . . they walk. They pass a block from Eddie's house. Worm wonders who won the fight.

She clutches him tighter. He can feel her breast against his shoulder. She's thinking of Pooter. But holding on to Worm. He's glad they're out here in the burbs, fewer people to see him in the hat. Her earlobe is pierced but has no earring. Her face is dazzling. He wonders if ghosts get sunburn. She wears no makeup. Like Claire Meeson.

She speaks. "Like I said, I'm not prom queen material. Him, he'll be prom king, you wait and see." She looks away. "We would have been seniors next year." She seems to be inspecting the neighborhood. "So for the last couple weeks of summer, I'm like, 'Why me?' Y'know? He could have anybody. And at that time I wasn't real big on self-esteem. So it took me a while to get over it. Like, 'Wow, what a lucky girl am I! Do I deserve this?'

"By the time school started in September, I figured I did. Not in a cocky, entitled way. It's like naturally, while we were talking . . . talking . . . we became three. Him. Me. Us. We liked the same shows. We finished each other's sentences. We were both terrified of thousand-leggers. Even the way our differences balanced out. His confidence. My doubts. His cool. My temper. We weren't the same. That wouldn't be good. But we meshed. We fit."

She turns to Worm, leans in, and tilts her face till she's under the hat brim too. She nose-bumps him. "Someday you'll fit, Worm. You'll surprise some girl. You'll surprise yourself. She'll call you Robbie." She laughs out loud. "Hah!"

"What?" says Worm.

"Names. H.D. Har. That's what everybody called him."

"Yeah?"

"Well, I changed all that. The world can thank"—she thumbs her chest—"*me.*"

"What do you mean?"

"Y'know," she says, "it's obvious from here. It was the moment I started to feel I really belonged, I was a full partner in us."

She waits, seems to want a prompt.

"When?" he says. "How?"

She giggles. "When I named him Pooter." She lets go of Worm, twirls past two houses, comes back to him. "I told him, 'People think you're perfect. We need to mess you up.' He says, 'Be my guest.'"

She told him he needed a nickname, but not an impressive one. A silly one. A nickname that would knock him off his pedestal.

"I thought about it for a week. Went through a hundred names. Then I remembered a little kid who used to live next to us. Just over being a baby, learning to talk, walk. He was being potty-trained. He got so he knew what he was doing, he just hadn't gotten the hang of controlling it. So he was still toddling around in diapers. And whenever he had to do number two, well, he would just go ahead and do number two. And then he would get all proud and toddle up to the nearest grown-up and point to his diaper and say, all proud, 'Poot.' And there it was." She laughs. "Hey—even *I* wasn't gonna call him Poop.

"So I told him to kneel before me. I put my hand on the top of his head and I said, 'I name thee Pooter Dean Baker.'"

"What did he think?" Worm says.

She laughs some more. "He loved it. He got it. Like, how could anyone take somebody named Pooter seriously? See, I knew what a lot of others didn't: he hated the pedestal. He wasn't perfect and he knew it.

"All you had to do was pay attention to him for five minutes, and you could figure that out. Like, he bit his fingernails. He was afraid of water. He couldn't swim! And the turtle! Second day after he got his driver's license? Ran over a turtle. Not because he was speeding. Because he'd just gotten a text and he took a second—just a second—to look down at his phone. Not to text back but just to see who it was. And he looks back up and there's the turtle in his rearview. Killed it. I held his hand. I told him about my fireflies. We teared up. Together."

She looks wistfully into the distance. "That was the day, the night. The new name, the turtle, the fireflies, crying together. We became us." She shakes her head, smiles at something only she can see. "The times we had . . ."

The mood is changing. Worm feels the name story is unfinished. "So," he says, "Pooter. How'd it go? I mean, with everybody else?"

She snaps her fingers. "No problem. He told his buddies to start calling him Pooter, and by October even the teachers were tempted to call him that, you could tell. Of course"—she laughs—"all the silly name did was make him more popular. Lovable."

He can't believe they're going to walk all the way to the cabins.

She repeats: "The times we had . . ." She takes a deep breath, the exhale nothing but pain. *Here it comes*, he thinks. "It was my fault, Worm. You have to understand that." She's looking at him, expecting a response. He nods. "*My* fault. Him. My parents. Three people. Three people who loved me standing over me in a cemetery. *I* did that. Me. Understand?"

He croaks, "Yeah."

"So . . . couples"—she swallows—"couples. There's a thing they usually do. Some little thing special to them. Secret. Maybe it's a signal you give each other as you pass in the hallway after third period. Maybe it's something you stick in each other's locker every day. Hooking little fingers. It can be silly. Even stupid. That's not the point. See what I'm saying?"

Sort of. He nods. "Uh-huh."

"So our secret little thing was this. Every morning when I woke up, first thing I did was reach for my phone and text him an emoji. Nothing else. Just that."

"Which one?" he says.

"The one with the red heart and a littler heart sort of floating above it? We liked to think it meant our one big blended heart had a little baby heart. Weren't we adorable?"

He nods again.

"And then each night the last thing *he* did before *he* went to bed was text our emoji to *me*. Sometimes I was still awake, but even if I was sleeping, I'd hear it come in and see it and go back to sleep with a smile on my face."

Not in any organized way or anything, Worm has lately been collecting boy-girl romance stuff he might want to make use of when the time comes for him. Keeps them in a little box in his head. He adds the two-hearted emoji.

"Starting around the end of October, every day and night. The bookends of my life. Us confirmed."

She lets go of his arm, puts a little distance between them. This bothers him, though he doesn't know why. Sometimes she's right down on his level, seems to get him as well as Eddie does. Other times he's reminded that she's three grades ahead of him. She inhabits a world he sees only as a dark portal.

"Then . . ." She takes a deep breath. "The twenty-third of December. When I got home from school, there were already flurries. It was going to be a major snow dump. Not that I cared. For me Christmas would begin on December twenty-sixth. That's because Pooter would be away both Christmas Eve and Christmas Day. Every year the family spent those two days with his grandparents somewhere way up in New York State. But that wasn't the worst of it. Cell phone reception between there and back home stunk, Pooter said. You were lucky to get through one out of ten times. We probably wouldn't be able to text or talk.

"How I treasured the emoji he sent me that night! In fact, he sent me a whole *screenful* of double hearts. I went to sleep clutching my iPhone like a teddy bear.

"The snow was a foot deep and still coming down when I woke up late Christmas Eve morning. My father is one of those snow-shovel fanatics. He doesn't wait till it stops snowing. He's out there in the driveway shoveling away while it's piling up again behind him. He has some complicated man-reason that my mom and I never understood.

"Meanwhile, Pooter, I figured, was already halfway to New York.

"I spent Christmas Eve day wrapping gifts and reading and moping and missing my Pooter. Every half hour I tried calling or texting him. No luck. And no buzzes from him.

"Looking back, I can see how it happened. With every failed text, I got a little more frustrated. The more I failed, the more I wanted to make contact. So by the time I went to bed, I was ready to *run* to New York. But something else occurred to me—and it was brilliant.

"I got my old little-kid snow shovel from the basement. I didn't bother to change: pj's, slippers. I put on my dad's long winter overcoat. I put the present in a pocket. (I'll get to that in a minute.) I got my boots from the closet and threw them in the car. I'd put them on when I got there. I snuck my father's car down the driveway, already shoveled except for a couple inches. Thanks, Dad!

"There was a glaze on the moonlit snow. The storm had finished with sleet. Meaning sharp edges for trench diggers. Perfect.

"Every station on the car radio was saying how cold it was going to be for the next couple days. Perfect.

"'Don't drive unless you have to,' the radio was saying. Well, I had to.

"The snowplows were out. The salt slingers were out. I went slow, crunching the salt. Careful . . . careful . . . be cool. . . .

"Pooter's house was normally fifteen minutes from mine. This would take longer. No problem. The whole point was to get there—I was actually giggling in the car at the thought of it. When I got to his house, I would put on my boots. I would take my little red shovel and, using my legendary artistic talents, I would trench-dig the world's biggest double-heart emoji in the snow. And big it would be because they have a massive front yard."

"What about the present?" says Worm.

She pokes him. "Thanks for the reminder. The present I would put in the middle of the big heart. Guess what it was."

"A puppy."

"Duct tape."

He snaps his fingers. "Yeah, dumb me. What else?"

"I'm serious," she says. "Remember I told you he said we needed some duct tape to shut us up that first night?"

He gets it. "A joke present."

"A joke present. The serious one was back in my room. An oatmeal-colored Irish wool cable-knit cardigan with a shawl collar."

"Impressive," he says, not that he would know one sweater from another.

"But the snow emoji, *that* was the thing." She laughs. "I kept picturing how it was probably going to go. As they pull in the driveway, one of his parents says, 'Hey, somebody was sledding in our yard.' And Pooter looks . . . and he knows . . . he *knows* instantly. He knows no way was I gonna let some cell phone problem stop me from sending the emoji. And he laughs and laughs, and maybe he tells his parents and maybe he doesn't, but whatever, he jumps out of the car and walks around the lopsided hearts, laughing and loving his lopsided girlfriend more than ever."

She says nothing now. They walk for blocks. Worm's tempted to turn his head and look at her, but he can't. He wants to hold her hand, but he knows she's with somebody else now. He knows she's probably in the last good moment of her life and she doesn't want to leave.

But she does.

"So I'm crunching along, only car out, and about half-way to his house the road is blocked. Flashing lights. A guy in a yellow vest is waving two red-capped flashlights cross-wise. I stop. I roll down the window. He looks at me funny.

"'Do you absolutely *have* to be out, miss?' he says.

"'Yes, I do,' I tell him.

"'Well,' he says. He shifts his eyes and tilts his head down the street, and for the first time I notice a car upside down on the sidewalk. Not to mention an ambulance and a bunch of police cars. For some reason what really strikes me is that the upside-down car's headlights are still on. The vest man clears his throat and he goes, 'I think the best thing now is to turn around and go back home, miss, and stay there.' He puts both hands on the roof and practically leans into the window. 'Please.'

"'OK,' I say. I back up and turn around. This was the worst part of my driver's test. It takes me about ten back-and-forths. Embarrassing.

"So I drive off, but I don't go home. I take a turn first chance I get. After all this, no way Pooter is not gonna get that emoji. There's not much else I'm sure of. Until now I've been drunk on my incredible idea. . . ."

Which is when, brilliantly, Worm's mother decides it's a good time to text him:

> Where are you?????
> I cant do it all!!!!
> NOW!!!!!!!!!!!!!!!!

Yeah, Mom, I'm gonna give up the most unbelievable experience in human history for a toilet brush. He shuts down his cell.

"The salty crunch is gone and there's no streetlights out here and the road no longer feels connected to the steering wheel. I'm more skating than driving. And I don't know where I am. I'm all turned around.

"OK . . ." She takes a deep breath, blinks, swallows. She's reliving it, she's back in the car. "OK—the house is over there"—she flaps her left arm—"somewhere. I gotta keep that in mind. Keep my bearings. I know the name of his street. I know the address. I just need to keep turning left, and sooner or later I'll circle back to it."

She kicks a mailbox post. "But it's not happening. The road keeps taking me right, and when it finally dead-ends at a crossroad at the bottom of a hill, I go sailing right through the stop sign because there's no salt"—she punches him—"there's *no salt.* You understand, Worm?" Another punch. He understands, but he can't speak. "There's no salt and no light and it's all hills and the *nose* of my father's car is sticking into a *snowbank.*

"I do the only three things I can. I put the car in reverse, I press the gas pedal, and I pray. It works. I back out. I'm on the road again, loster than ever. Up, down. Up, down. Never saw so many hills. I'm using the brakes as little and as gently as possible. I know about that. I'm even using the trick my father told me: for better traction I'm driving with the right tires off the road, where it's crunchier.

"I'm feeling pretty good about my snow-driving skills when I find myself at the top of a hill that isn't curvy at all. It's perfectly straight. But long. My high beams don't reach the bottom. I stop. My foot's on the brake. And the car starts moving anyway. It's on its own, weaving, pirouetting, dancing with the ice. . . ." She laughs. "There shoulda been waltz music." She waves her hands back and forth. "La-dah-dah-de-dah . . . turning and turning and going faster and faster, and I'm thinking, 'Screw what they say, I'm hitting the brake,' and I'm practically standing on the pedal with both feet, and now the car isn't dancing, it's decided it's just gonna go straight down—*backward*—and suddenly right there on the windshield is the man in the yellow vest, and he's crying and he's saying to me, '*Please . . . please . . . ,*' and I'm turning the wheel like a NASCAR driver and pounding the brakes, and it works and now the car is turning . . . turning . . . and just as it finishes turning and the man in the yellow vest goes away, here comes the tree."

They walk. Many blocks pass. He hears birds. He thinks someday he should get a DVD or go online and find out what calls belong to what birds. Because he can never see them.

She wanders away from him. Back and forth across the street. Across front yards. Once she disappears down an alley and doesn't show up for another ten minutes. He just keeps walking.

Eventually she comes back to him.

"It was my fault. Say it, Worm."

Is this a game?

"*Say* it. 'It was your fault, Becca Finch.'"

"It was your fault."

"Becca Finch."

"Becca Finch."

"You stupid jackass."

"You stupid jackass." He means it.

She punches him. His left shoulder is getting sore. "Look what I did." Another punch. "Do you *understand?*"

He punches her back. "I understand."

"I left three people at the grave. Two parents and a boyfriend. Devastated. Because of *me.* Because I wouldn't listen. To the warnings. To the ice. To the upside-down car. To the man in the yellow vest. To my own common sense." She stops, faces him, shakes him by the shoulders, yells. "Why, Worm? *Why?* Why did I destroy three lives? Four, counting me."

"You were stupid."

"I know . . . I know. . . ." She's sobbing into his sore shoulder.

She pops up with an ugly laugh. "And *when,* Worm? Hah! Don't tell *me* I don't have a great sense of timing. When, Worm? When, of *all* the nights in the year, did I decide to send the three people on earth who loved me most to the cemetery? *When,* Worm?"

130

He barely chokes it out: "Christmas Eve." And thinks: *I'll never call them Wrappers again.*

Something hits him in the side of the face. There's a cigarette on the ground, still burning. High school kids are curbing them in a rusty convertible.

"Waddaya think this is, Deader? A fashion show?"

"Black shirt not enough for ya? Ya gotta do the loser hat too? Feather? Ya *girl*!"

Another cigarette comes flying and the car takes off and he starts breathing again. Becca is squatting in the street, giving them a double-finger salute. "Here's yer loser hat, ya losers!"

Worm thinking: *Where's that side of her been hiding?*

She comes to him, smiling. "So . . . want me to take the hat back?"

Yes! he thinks. "No," he says. He's thought about pulling out the yellow feather but can't even do that.

Suddenly she grabs his wrist, looks at his watch. . . .

Becca smacks her own hand. "Bad Becca."

"What?" Worm says.

"I'm supposed to be here for you—to fix you—and all I'm doing is talking about my own stupid self."

"I like to listen," he tells her, and adds, "I don't need fixing."

"I'll be the judge of that." She takes his arm again, perks back to girlfriend mode. "And I bet you'd rather watch than do."

She's right. He's known this about himself for a while, but he didn't think it showed. He's felt guilty about it. The world is run by people who *do*.

"O . . . K," she says, looking into him. "Acme—"

"Acne."

132

". . . is the tragedy of your life."

He wouldn't have put it *that* way.

"Best friend: Eddie . . . Eddie . . ."

"Fusco."

"Fusco. Fave color, red. Food, oyster stew." She side-eyes him. "Sticking with that?"

He holds up his hand. "Swear."

She points at him. "Shy. Hates attention." He waits, senses more coming. She grins, finger-flicks the hat brim. "And yet makes a spectacle of himself on the street, broad daylight." Turns away while pointing back at him, proclaims: "Ladies and gentlemen! Behold! Worm Tarnauer wears a hat!"

Yeah, he's mortified. But not as much as he would have been yesterday.

"You're brave," she says.

He doesn't believe it. But he'll tuck it away, look at it later.

"Sorry," she says. "I'm rushing it, I know. So . . . girlfriend. Have one?"

"No."

"Ever?"

"No."

"If I was boss of the world and said you must pick one right now, who would it be? Quick, don't think."

"Claire Meeson."

She nods. "Claire Meeson. You like her."

He shrugs. "You said pick somebody. Don't think."

"She likes you?"

"Prob'ly not," he says.

She gives a small nod and a grin that says, *That tells me all I need to know.*

She strikes a thinking pose, finger to chin. "OK. Let's see what we have here. Pimples . . . shy . . . listener . . . watcher . . . aspiring kisser . . . Eddie Fusco . . . Claire . . ." She studies him some more, points. "Eddie. He's not like you, right?"

What's she getting at? He shrugs.

"He's . . . hmm . . . outgoing, right? Life of the party. Mr. Popular."

"I guess," he says, thinking, *Like Pooter.*

"And you'd like to be like him."

Absolutely. And remembers this morning's uncomfortable visit to Eddieworld. "Not sure," he says.

She studies him, fingertip-tapping her chin, nodding. "We might be onto something here, Wormolator."

She snatches the hat from his head. And suddenly he knows why he doesn't want to give it up. It keeps at least part of his face in shadow. He has learned to dread the merciless complexion-revealer of bright light. It's ninety-three million miles away, but he knows the sun is highlighting every cavernous pore and mountainous bump. Her finger is tapping her chin. He's never been stared at so intensely, so long.

Finally she speaks. "You know what I'm doing, Worm?"

"Not really."

"I'm looking at you." Doesn't he know it. "Making you uncomfortable, am I?"

He shrugs, concedes. "Kinda."

She plants the hat over his face. "That better?" she says.

Even Worm has his limits. He slaps the hat away. "What's your point?"

"The point is, those things don't stop you from being a good-looking kid." She runs her finger high on his cheek. "You have good bones."

Good bones? he thinks. *Who needs good bones? You can't see bones.*

She studies him some more. He's feeling like a—what?—zoo animal.

"You're into video games, right?"

"I guess."

"Hmm . . ." Studying . . . "And is there one especially that you love, you're nuts about?"

"Maybe," he says. And prays she doesn't ask him the name of it.

She stops to sniff a yellow flower, pulls a blade of grass, chews it, continues walking.

"OK . . . here's a question I had to answer once. If you had a choice of being one of three animals, which would it be? A turtle? An eagle? Or a cobra?"

He knows his answer instantly: turtle. But he's pretty sure it's wrong. Nobody messes with a cobra. King of snakes. Eagle. King of birds. Eddie would say cobra. "Cobra," he says.

She just gives a little nod, no sign whether he's right or wrong.

"Wha'd *you* say?" he asks her.

"Turtle," she says.

She stops. She faces him full body, grips both of his shoulders. "Worm . . . ," she says. "Robbie." No smile now. Only sadness in her eyes. "This is your life you're missing."

She's right. He knows this, though he never admits it to himself. Cobra. What was he thinking? He loves that she answered turtle.

She knuckle-knocks his head above his ear, like he's a door. "Knock-knock." He just stares at her. She megaphones her mouth, like she's calling from afar. "Come on out and play! You've been in there long enough!"

There was a time when he *was* out. *I'm a Little Teapot.*

"Worm," she says. "I want you to do something, OK?"

Yellow alert. "OK."

The raspberry fluffies she's been carrying, she drops

them at his feet. "Take off your sneaks and put these on," she says, but sees something in his face. "OK, scratch that," and slips her own bare feet into them.

She's thinking . . . thinking. . . . "OK, little steps. How about this?" She moonwalks up the sidewalk. The goofy slippers make it comical. "Your turn," she says.

He's torn. Moonwalk on a public sidewalk? Shy Worm Tarnauer?

He tries. He butchers it, of course. Probably the worst moonwalk of all time. He wants to crawl into the gutter. But even more he wants to please her—and apparently he is. She's stomping her foot and clapping: "Worm . . . Worm . . . Worm . . ." She applauds when he stops. She throws up her arms and cheers. He's glad nobody else can hear. They walk away, naturally.

Something on a front lawn gets her attention. "Can it be?"

She crosses the lawn, walks right up to a big gray pot holding a bush. She plucks a white flower from the bush, smells it, falls swooning to the ground, gets up, comes back, and sticks it under his nose. "Smell," she says.

He smells. He's smelled an occasional rose or Easter lily, but this is something else, like somewhere somebody left a window open and a whiff of paradise drifted in.

"You hardly see them up here," she says. "My aunt has

one in Florida." She gives him another sniff, takes the flower away, brings it back. "OK? Good?" He nods. She tosses it onto the lawn. "Gardenia," she says. "Remember that."

This is your life you're missing.

They walk. She talks, despite scolding herself for hogging the talk. She can't help herself, like his father. Which is cool with Worm. The listener.

She stops.

2:41 p.m.

Becca's looking to the right. At the entrance to the township park a block away.

"Is that what I think it is?" she says.

"It's a park," Worm says.

"You played there?"

"When I was little."

She grabs his hand. They run.

It's mostly grass. Ball fields. With a band shell and a pavilion and a grove for picnics and a playground of color-ful stuff for little kids. His favorite was the sliding board. He's disappointed it's not here. The one here now is the same color as before—green—and curved, but it's much smaller, not the thrilling toboggan ride down the Alps that he recalls.

"Swings!" she chirps, and they do the swings, see who

can go higher. The structure shimmies, warning them it's not for people their size.

Merry-go-round! They jump on. She pushes off with her foot like on an old-school scooter, so for him it's a free ride. Everything was a free ride when he was little. His father pulled him in a sled down unplowed roads.

They hang upside down by their knees on the monkey bars. He feels blood falling to his head. He never used to notice.

The sliding board. She goes first. It's so small that, as she sits at the top, her legs come practically down the whole thing. Her slide is over in a moment.

He climbs the green steps. Stands at the top, barely higher than his own height. And it's coming back to him. The view is the same as before . . . the merry-go-round straight ahead, pavilion to the right . . . the plastic green slide curving down and away . . . and something astonishing occurs to him. It's not a new sliding board. It's the same old one. So tame now. So safe. So small. Not the screamingly treacherous plunge of his memory. The slide hasn't changed. He has.

"Remembering?" she says.

"Sorta," he says. And kinda wants to tell her but decides to keep it to himself for the time being: standing atop the dizzy-high sliding board one day and surveying everything below and the spinning and swinging kids and feeling . . .

what? . . . Grand? . . . Majestic? . . . And spreading his legs and pounding his tiny fists on his tiny chest and sending out a Tarzan yell that he imagined reached every ear in the jungle.

"Once you were King Worm," she says, and she bows as if he still is, and down he comes.

3:18 p.m.

Back on the sidewalk.

"That was nice," Becca says. "But that was yesterday." She gives a sigh—a real, out-loud sigh, like if you were writing it, you'd spell it out, maybe underline it.

It takes a minute, but Worm gets it. She's supposed to fix him and she's not doing it. She's flunking. And he's not doing anything to help (unless you count the sick moonwalk). He loves that she's here but hates that he's her assignment. He hates himself for letting her down, for making her job impossible by refusing to be anything but the old Worm. He feels rotten.

"I'm sorry," he says.

She gives him a quick look and keeps walking. He hates her silence. She's been chatty and gushy all day, but she's

142

no match for the Watching Worm, the Worm Without a Voice, the Worm Who Can't Speak First.

He blurts: "I see black bears."

She stops, faces him. She tries a smile but doesn't get far. Her shoulders dip, just enough to show she knows she's lost the game but she's being a good sport. "Nice," she says. "Good for you." She resumes walking.

He needs questions to get her back to herself. But what can he ask that doesn't bring up the life that for her is now over?

Do you think you'll go back to the bottle?

Could you see God from in there?

What can he do to perk her up?

"I meet writers," he says. "They stay in our cabins."

The thin smile is gone. "I know. You told me."

"That's where they write."

Mock surprise: "Really? I thought they came to shoot bears."

He recalls the text from his mother. . . . "You like to read?"

He can see the answer from her smirk. Good. "Yes, Worm, I like to read."

What was the name . . . Daze . . . ?

"Ever hear of Daisy somebody?"

She stops like she's hit a wall. She's nothing but eyes. "Daisy *Chimes*?"

"Yeah, her," he says.

She grabs him by the shoulders. She's under his hat brim. "Day . . . zee . . . Chimes?"

He prays he's right. How many Daisy writers can there be? "Yeah. I think."

She's shaking him; she's strong. "*Daisy Chimes* is staying in one of *your* cabins?"

"I think so," he says.

"Right *now*?"

He looks at his watch. "Yeah, I guess. We usually only see them at meals. Sometimes not even then. Sometimes I have to deliver all three meals to their cabins because they don't even want to take time out to come over and eat." Many have come for a week, and he's seen nothing but the backs of their cars when they leave. Funky bunch, writers.

She backs off, tilts her head, sly-eyes him. "You don't even know who Daisy Chimes is, do you?"

He never should've brought this up. "Sure. She's a writer."

"Wha'd she write?" Challenging him.

"I forget," he says. "I'm not big on titles."

She grins. "You're not big on reading either." She pokes him. "Are you?"

"I go to school, don't I? Everybody reads."

144

She nods. "Yeah. And when you're home, you're at that video game you love, right? What's it called?"

"I didn't say."

"So say."

"Nuke 'Em ALL Now!"

When he says it to her, it sounds different. Not like he feels when he's playing it.

"Sounds like fun," she says. She's not serious.

She grins, drapes an arm around his shoulders. "Daisy Chimes, my dear Wormlet, is only one of the world's great writers. She's *only* my favorite writer of *all time.*"

Worm's discomfort vanishes. He's made her happy. Gardenia petals are falling inside him.

"She just came today," he tells her. "They usually come on Monday."

"I want to meet her." She says it just like that. Like she's not dead.

"They can't be disturbed. It's our biggest rule."

She stares at him, beams. "Dinner!"

"*If* she comes," he says. "She's prob'ly one of those hermits." When he delivers their meals, he's supposed to leave the tray at the door, knock twice, and get outta there.

"But she *might* come."

He's torn between wanting to make her happy and the

terror of an impossible dinner scene. *Excuse me, folks. I have a ghost here who wants to meet one of you.*

Before he can respond, she's at him again, shaking him. His shoulders are getting sore. "Is there a bookstore around here?"

"Used," he says. He can't remember the name. He points behind them, to town.

She starts pulling him. He digs in his heels. "Wait!" He looks at the nearest street sign. "It's, like, a mile. More."

She pulls. "Right. So let's go."

He drops to a squat, like a catcher, smacks her hand. "I gotta be home. I was supposed to be home right after school. My dad's gone today. I'm s'posed to be cleaning eight toilets about now. Changing eight beds. Pretty soon I have to deliver meals. We don't have *time* to go back there. I keep telling you, we live in the *boondocks*."

She squats beside him. Her voice is calm. "Worm," she says, "I must—*must*—get a copy of *Wendy Wins*. That's my favorite book by my favorite author. Then I want Daisy Chimes to sign it for me. 'To Becca.' Then I can go back to the bottle happy forever. Got it?"

"I'm out of money," he says.

"No problem," she says. "I'll steal it. I've done it before."

"You steal books?" he says.

"Tootsie Rolls," she says.

She stands. She smiles down at him. She starts walking toward town.

Book . . . author . . . sign . . .

And here it is, right in front of him the whole time, a brilliant play that will be his forever gift to her.

"Wait!" he calls.

Becca stops, waits.

"What if they don't have it?" Worm says. "What if *we* do? My parents . . . when a writer signs up to come . . . if there's a book they wrote . . . my parents try to get the book and have it there when the writer shows up so the writer can sign it. There's three shelves full of them in the dining room."

You could swim in her eyes. "You think?"

"What's it called? *Wendy* . . ."

"*Wendy Wins.*"

"Is it, like, her most famous book? Everybody knows it?"

"Millions."

"There's a coffee table for the new ones." He grins. "I bet it's sitting there."

Her grin matches his, but only for a moment. "It changed my life," she says.

"It's yours."

3:38 p.m.

Worm and Becca are walking. She's talking.

"When we get there, will they be having dinner?"

He looks at his watch. "Maybe. Probably." Even then they'll have to run, but he's holding off on that.

"So how it goes is, you just do whatever it is you do, and I'll just stand there and gawk at Daisy Chimes, watch every bite, every sip."

"What if she's not there?" he says. "What if she gets her dinner in her cabin, one of those?"

"Fine. You deliver it and—guess what—we're in the cabin."

Another glance at the watch. "We'll get there too late. She'll already be eating. And don't think about pickup. They leave their dinner trays outside the door. So nobody bothers them. I told you."

"Even better," she says. She drapes her arm around his shoulders, sisterly. "Trust me, Worm—you are *going* to bother her. You are going to snatch her book from the coffee table and march into her cabin and tell her to sign it for Becca."

Worm can't imagine himself doing all that. On the other hand, he can't imagine Becca Finch not getting what she wants.

They walk. She talks. He listens.

She tells him stories, from her first memories on. It's all pretty ordinary. No fireflies. No Pooter. No trauma. Life in Elwood, PA.

Worm is loving it. He wishes his house was even farther away, wishes it would pick itself up and move another ten miles down the road. He's over feeling like he's letting her down. *You need to fix me? Well, good luck.* Worm hereby pledges to be perfectly, totally Worm, to not deviate an inch from his Wormness, to make her have to work her assignment as hard and long as possible—because an icy stab to the heart tells him what he's probably known all along: that as soon as she fixes him, she's gone.

They walk.

5:59 p.m.

Worm doesn't hear the car. Doesn't know it's there till the bumper and grille slide into his side vision. The faint *shhh* of a window rolling down . . . a voice . . . his father's. "Nice hat."

Not a car. His father's pickup.

"Who?" Becca says.

He whispers to her, "My dad."

They stop.

"That was a strange couple of seconds there," says his dad, his voice friendly as always but something else too, relief maybe. The door lock button pops up. "I see this kid walking down the street. No big hurry. Like, cabin dinner delivery? What's that? Change the linens? What's that? From the ears down everything says it's the kid I'm looking for, it's my Worm. Black shirt, check. Height, check.

Old-school sneaks, check. But the *hat* . . . the *feather.* I'll take a wild guess that somebody has had an interesting day."

Worm is not sure how to play this, prays his father doesn't go federal case.

The door swings open. "Come on," he says, still friendly. "Dinner's on."

There's a problem. The back seat is filled with stuff: lamps, pictures. Where's Becca going to fit?

"Aunt Rita's stuff," his father explains. "No room in her new place. Let's go."

Worm feels a push from behind, and next thing he knows, he's in the passenger seat with the ghost or whatever of Becca Finch in his lap. She feels exactly like what she is—or was: 130 pounds and five feet seven inches of girl, heavy on his thighs, now twisting and sticking her finger in his ear and tickling him through his sweaty black shirt. He can't help it, he giggles.

"While you're busy laughing," says his dad, looking at him through Becca, "if you'll be so kind as to shut the door and put your seat belt on, I can proceed to drive us home to one extremely unhappy mother."

Worm shuts the door. The seat belt won't go around them both . . . duh, she doesn't need one. The truck speeds up. The girl won't give him a break. She continues to play with his face—ears, nose, mouth—like babies do with grown-ups. And now she goes too far. She drills her little finger up his left nostril. He smacks her hand away.

"Fly in here?" his father says.

"Yeah," says Worm. "*Big* one."

She shakes with laughter in his lap.

While Becca plays with his face, his dad fills the rest of the ride with chatter about moving day with Aunt Rita. Worm tries not to be too obvious about keeping his hand over his nose. He will *not* let that finger go up there again.

Worm's mom is at the kitchen counter getting des-
serts ready when they walk in the back door. She doesn't
even look up. Hell hath no fury like a mother whose texts
have been ignored all day. Well, better this than getting hol-
lered at.

In the dining room, around the big table, the dinnertime writers ignore him too. They're just eating away, chat-
ting to each other, as if he's not even . . .

And now he gets it. *Clever, Mom.* She's using the Dead
Wednesday thing to cover her fury at him. She's told the
writers about it, told them to act as if he's not there, because the black shirt means he's dead. Which is pretty
funny when you think about it. While the eating writers are
pretending they can't see him, they *really* can't see *her.*

There are six women, one man.

Becca whispers in his ear, excited: "I don't see her. Get the book."

He leads her into the living room . . . to the coffee table . . . it's there! She squeals. He grabs it—then she grabs it and bops on out the front door.

He comes to his senses, follows her outside.

"We can't," he says.

"We can," she says. "We will."

"No," he says. "You can't bother them in their cabins. It's rule number one. It's gotta be some other way."

Becca thinks on it. "She's eating. That's not as uninterruptible as writing." She pulls him along. "She'll be cool. We're readers."

He wrenches free. "No!" He's in enough trouble already.

She lets go of him, looks at him. The urgency falls from her face, her posture. She smiles. "OK, Worm," she says. "I've been dragging you along most of the day. Calling the shots. 'Say this, Worm. Do that, Worm.' How are you supposed to man up if I don't turn you loose?"

She spreads her arms, takes three steps back. "There. You're free. It's the Night of the New Worm. I'm leaving you with two words. That's all. Are you looking at me?"

Is he. He nods.

"Be bold," she says. "Be. Bold."

She walks away.

The cabins are arranged in two half-moons—four and four—facing each other across the meadow. Each writer's name is computer-printed on a card tucked into a tag holder beside the door. Worm and Becca look at every name tag before they come to it on the last cabin, #8: DAISY CHIMES.

Worm is right beside her but still terrified. He thought *bold* meant "fearless."

They step onto the narrow, planked porch. They're standing at her door. *Be bold* is fading fast. *Stall!*

"Tootsie Rolls?" he says.

She grins. "Perfect crime. Tell you later. Now knock."

"What do I say?" he whispers.

She shoves the book into his hand. "Tell her you're a big fan. Massive fan. You live here. Work here. You're totally sorry to bother her at dinner, but you simply *cannot* allow your favorite writer of all time to come and go without getting her autograph. 'This book changed my life.' Say that."

"That's dumb. It's about a *girl*."

"She'll like you even more. Enlightened man." Her eyes are flashing. "Make a fist." He makes a fist. She grabs him by the wrist, knocks his fist—way too loud—upon the cabin door.

Why should this day of surprises stop now? Worm expects a youngish person fitting the name Daisy, but when the door opens, he finds himself facing an old lady. She's wearing a pink-and-green bathrobe, each bare foot has a toe ring, and a rope of braided white hair hangs over her shoulder, almost to her waist. She's no taller than him.

"Well, hello," she says. She's looking right at him— boldly, like Becca does—and smiling in a way that seems to say, *Chill, dude, I'm not gonna bite you.*

"Hullo?" he says brilliantly.

There's a stick pen in her hand. He's interrupted her writing, not her dinner. On the desk behind her sit a soup bowl and a half-eaten roll. He wants to turn and run.

She glances down at the book in his hand, and the smile, if anything, gets bigger. "Like to come in?" She backs up.

Becca pinches him on the butt. He steps into the room.

He wishes he could ask Becca what to say. He and

the writer stare at each other for about nineteen hours. "So . . . ," says Daisy Chimes, "I've heard there's a Robbie on the premises. Would that be you?"

"Yes." He adds, "Ma'am."

Becca whispers, "Say you're sorry."

"I'm sorry," he says.

"For not bringing your dinner."

"For not bringing your dinner."

"I was busy with a ghost."

"I was late getting home." Hears a giggle.

Daisy Chimes dismisses his apology with a wave of her hand. "Well, some dinner angel left it at my door. The soup was wonderful. My compliments to the chef. That would be your mother?"

He nods.

"And tell your parents what a wonderful, cozy place they have here. It's everything I'd heard. Sometimes you just need to get away from the hubbub."

Hubbub?

He's not sure what the right response is. He takes a shot: "Thanks."

She taps his wrist with the stick pen. "Something tells me that's one of my books."

"Yeah," he says. *"Wendy Wins."* Duh.

"And let me guess," she says. "You'd like me to sign it."

"Oh . . . yeah." He hands it to her. Remembers his manners. "Please. Thank you."

His head remains empty, but his nerves are calming down. He's lived at Writers' Re-Treat all his life, and this is the most time he's ever spent with one of them.

"No problem," she says. Both hands fall to her sides and she starts chuckling, shaking her head. "I find myself saying that all the time. 'No problem . . . no problem.' Where did 'You're welcome' go?" She's looking at him as if he's got the answer.

"No problem," he says.

She slaps her chest with the book and bends over, laughing. Behind him, Becca is cracking up.

For a busy writer, Daisy Chimes seems in no hurry to kick him out. He wonders if his parents have ever actually talked to one of these people.

"O . . . K . . . ," she says at last, spilling a few final laugh drips. She sits at the desk and opens the book to the title page. She looks at him. "So . . . 'To Robbie'?"

For a moment he's confused. A hard pinch on the butt quickly de-confuses him. "Uh, no—'To Becca'? Please."

She looks up. There's a new delight in her eyes. "Ah . . . Becca. Two *c*'s, yes?"

Becca whispers, "Yes!"

"Yes," he says.

She starts signing. He remembers, says it: "This book changed my life."

The pen stops. She looks up. The delight is surprisy now. "And you a boy, no less. Call me thrilled."

Butt pinch.

"Well, I mean . . . ," he bumbles, "her too. It changed Becca's life. Totally. She loves you."

She gives him a slow look. The half-gone bowl of soup must be cold by now. He hopes he doesn't get grilled about Becca. With her free hand she touches his. "You give Becca a hug for me, OK?"

He nods. "OK."

She finishes signing:

With love,
Daisy Chimes

She holds out her hand. He shakes it. "Thank you, Robbie, for stopping by. This has been a sweet moment."

What does he say to that? Becca is tugging him. He smiles, nods, turns to go.

Becca blocks him at the door. She looks frantic. She whispers rat-a-tat in his ear.

He turns. The writer is still looking at him. He sends her a stupid smile. "Uh . . ." He holds up the book. "Wendy?"

She nods, smiles. "Yes?"

"Uh, what she wins?"

"Yes?"

"She wins, like . . . herself, right?"

Daisy Chimes gives him two thumbs-ups. "Bingo."

Becca smacks him on the rump. "Yes!"

He sends the writer another stupid smile and a wave and escapes cabin #8.

6:40 p.m.

In the years to come Worm will many times try and fail to recall every moment of the following hours, which he will designate *In the Woods*. As to the order of moments, he will never be certain of any but the last.

He will achingly regret not switching the phone in his pocket to record. The only regret-deleting strategy that will work is to tell himself that the phone would not have captured Becca's voice anyway. Sometimes he will believe it.

As he recalls those hours over and over, he will find that the moments seem to cluster into distinct groupings, to which, in time, he will assign titles. By the end of high school he will be calling them chapters.

Every ten seconds she stares at the title page, where Daisy Chimes signed her name. Her face is all smile and marvel. "I can't believe it," she keeps saying. "I *cannot* believe it."

"How'd it change your life?" he asks her.

They're only a minute or two into the woods and already deeper than he's ever gone.

"It gave me permission to be myself," she says.

Worm thinking: *Permission?* He knows he's not one of the great ones. He knows he's shy and quiet and hangs on the sidelines. But it's never occurred to him that he's not who he is. He's never felt he had to consult some book to ask if it's OK for him to be himself.

"You needed *permission?*"

"It's hard to explain to someone who's as comfortable with themselves as you are," she says. "I always kinda felt like I needed to apologize. I walk in front of somebody. 'I'm sorry.' I take a seat in front of somebody at a movie. 'I'm sorry.' I mean, sure, I did plenty of stuff I *should* be sorry for, and I was. But a lot of it wasn't real. It was just in my head, a game called I'm Sorry. I was probably no worse than anyone else."

Worm nods, thinks. "Starting with the fireflies?"

She smiles, nudges him. "Yeah. As good a starting place as any."

"And so Wendy," he says, "how did she fix you?"

"She took 'I'm sorry' out of my life. She taught me it was OK to be imperfect. 'Be bold.' I say it to you? She's the one who said it to me. Or Daisy Chimes, actually. She put the words in Wendy's mouth—she screams them out her bedroom window—and Wendy gave them to me."

"And now me," he says. Thinking: *I gotta read this book.* "So," he says, "by the time you met Pooter . . ."

"I was ready. I was changed. I was me. Surprised? Yeah. But . . . what? Undeserving? No. Before we walked out of lunch at Waldo's, I knew. I didn't care if he *did* go back to check on another chick. I was keeping him." She holds out her fist. He bumps it.

····· **Daddy Longlegs** ·····

She wanders now. He follows at a distance. It's a strange world out here, a setting for stories his mother read to him when he was little. Any minute he half expects Hansel and Gretel to show up. They veer around trees. There's a smell here in the woods that you don't get near the house. *Nature,* he figures.

She squeals, dashes, kneels, scoops.

When she turns, she's got something on the back of her hand. A spider. A pea walking on eight stilty threads. Worm backs off.

"Daddy longlegs," she says.

"Spider," he says.

"Harmless," she says.

She lets it crawl up her arm . . . onto her shoulder . . . her ear!

"You're creeping me out," he tells her.

She reaches up, gives the bug a ride down. "Hold out your hand."

"No," he says.

"Hold out your hand."

He holds out his hand. The bug crawls over her fingers and onto the back of his hand. *Stay there*, he prays. He feels eight tiny somethings on the skin of his hand. *If atoms had feet.*

"The legs never stop growing," she says. "So every once in a while, he'll bite off his feet so things don't get out of control."

"TMI," he says.

The bug begins to move, steps primly onto the cuff of his black shirt. He panics, shakes his arm. The spider falls to the ground.

She laughs, pats his head. "Such a brave Worm. Welcome to planet Earth, the world outside your head."

····· Touch ·····

She does a lot of that, touching. She's forever kneeling, sniffing, feeling, running her fingertips over moss and tree bark—he never knew it came in so many colors—dislodging stones and delighting at the crawly stuff coming out. One time she foots over a rock and picks up a little lizard. It's orange and black, about two inches long, slimy.

"Salamander," she says. "Because they're wet-looking, people used to think they could live in fire. So frying pans were called salamanders." She holds out her hand. "Here."

"No way," he says. This time she listens. She puts the lizard back.

In the same hand she takes his. They walk, dodge trees, hand in hand. Out of nowhere she whirls and kisses him, on the lips. Backs off, grins. "Ever kiss a girl? Besides your mother? Don't lie."

"Not really," he says. To anyone else he would lie.

She kisses him again, longer, harder, his cheeks cradled in her hands, which don't seem to notice the bumps. He is thoughtless. When she finally pulls away, the front flap of his endless hat brim is standing up like a lifted tablecloth.

····· Silence ·····

As he replays *In the Woods* in his head over the coming years, Worm will sometimes think it was all kisses and spiders and salamanders and feeling trees. But it wasn't. It was mostly silence. Or more truly, talklessness.

Whenever she's beside him, she holds his hand. Sometimes she interlaces her fingers with his. But it's never long before she's bolting to check out some new wonder:

"Fiddlehead fern!"

"Mayapples!"

They're hidden under leaves. She eats one, hands one to him. He tries it. Crunchy. Good.

"Raspberries!"

"Sassafras!" She bolts, plucks up a plant, waves the root under his nose.

He can't believe it. "Root beer."

"Sassafras," she says. "You can make your own root beer. See the leaf? Shaped like a mitten. That's how you know."

He has to ask: "What is it with you and all this nature stuff?"

She hugs his arm. "I just love it. I lived in a ticky-tack development. Springview Run. Has there *ever* been a more fake name?" She pirouettes. "This is where I wanted to live. I wanted to be you!"

And I want to live in town, he thinks. Or does he?

They return to the silence that is not silent. The silence that first tingled sweetly on his lips and now fills the forest. The silence that cannot contain this girl beside him, this girl that is a ghost that is a girl that is and was and that dances and dashes and laughs and fills him with *now.*

She jerks toward him, glares down at his wrist, his watch. "No!" she shouts, and tears the watch from his arm.

171

She drops to her knees and scoops at the dirt till there's a foot-deep hole. She drops the watch in and covers it up. She grabs his arm and catches his earlobe between her teeth and bites till it hurts, and they walk on in the silence that is louder than kettledrums.

····· **PJ's** ·····

It is during one of her mad bursts from him that he finally, after most of a day, connects two dots.

"You're wearing pajamas," he says.

She poses. "You noticed."

"It was December twenty-fourth."

She swoons. "I am in the presence of the world's greatest memory."

"It was cold."

"Freezing."

"Where's your father's coat you put on when you left the house?"

She wags a finger at him. "Ah . . . you caught me. I forgot to mention that our car has a fantastic heater, and it must have been on high and I was roasting in there, and I can't figure out how to make the heat go lower, so I shrug off my father's coat, which was of course a bad idea because I lost what little control I had of the car, and that's when I went sliding down the hill into the snowbank."

Two more dots: "So you're sorry for that too."

She jabs *Wendy* at him. "Bingo."

"And the boots were in the car."

"In the car. Waiting for me to execute my brilliant idea."

····· Brook ·····

The unsilent silence is marked by rustlings: their own footsteps, the rush of not-quite-seen animal things in the bushes. And now a new sound, a different kind of rustle.

"Water!" she cries, and sprints ahead. She's out of sight in seconds, and he hears, "Yahoo!"

He finds and picks up first one raspberry fluffie and now the other, and now here she is, standing ankle-deep in a brook, stream, whatever, so skinny he can jump across it. He's always heard it was out here somewhere, never bothered to look.

She's cupping her hands and drinking and swishing her hands around, and she picks up a rock in the water and screeches, "Crayfish!" And now she's on her knees, the water soaking all the way up her pj legs, and she's clutching at the streamside mud with her fingers; her fingers are claws ripping into the earth and raking mud and water into her hair, and she's pounding the mud and pounding the water, pounding and pounding with her fists and looking at

173

him and crying as loud as a girl can cry: "Oh, Robbie—I was only *seventeen*!"

····· "You Lied" ·····

He knows there is nothing he can say. If he was in a movie, he would probably squat in the water and pull her into his arms and stroke her muddy hair and go, "It's OK . . . it's OK. . . ."

At least he squats. He watches her watching him. His tears join hers. He cannot remember the silence. The shadows of the trees and the setting sun make a lacework on the forest floor.

In time she pulls herself up. He helps her from the water. He finger-rakes the bigger clumps of mud from her hair. She stands with her head bowed, like a patient child, lets him slip her fluffies back on.

The anger—how long has it been here? At least since the long walk. Lying low, biding its time, letting sympathy carry the load. Not now. Suddenly it's gorging him, demanding to be let out.

"You lied," he says.

She stops, her head jerks back, shocked.

"Huh?"

He snatches the book from her hand. "You said the book changed your life. Gave you . . . *permission*." He sneers the word. "You told me. You told Daisy Chimes. But you lied. You didn't change. Not really." He points in her face. "You're a fake changer."

She blinks, stares at him, her face streaked with mud. She's looking down at him, as always, but somehow seems smaller now.

He wags the book in her face. "You know how I know? Huh? Y'know?"

She shakes her head.

He screams into her face. "Because you're in that damn bottle. You got a couple more minutes here and then— *bam*—back to the bottle."

She's starting to cry. She lashes out at him. "Where I belong!"

He shoves her, so hard she lurches backward and falls on her butt. He straddles her. Yells. "See? *That's* the point! You're feeling sorrier for yourself than the whole cemetery of people at your funeral. Where you belong? Seriously? Even ghosts gotta chill, Finch."

He walks away, turns back. It all wants to come out at once. "Yeah, sure, it was your fault. Who's arguing? Your parents know it. Pooter knows it. The question is, where do you go from here? Unless you're in love with bottles."

He whips off the hat, plunks it on her head, pulls it down over her ears as she struggles to stand. "You're smart. You're funny. You taught me more in one afternoon than I learned in my whole life. You're still you, y'know, whatever you are. You're still Rebecca Finch." He thumps his chest. He sneers. "*Permission?* Screw Daisy Chimes. *I'm* giving you permission. Permission not to be pathetic. 'Oh, boohoo. I can still smell those bugs I killed.' Here she is, folks, our headline exhibit! Your once-in-a-lifetime chance to see . . . the amazing . . . the stupendous . . . MOPER IN A BOTTLE! Come one, come all! Seeing is believing! She mopes! She sulks! She pouts! She apologizes! For EVERYTHING! One measly quarter, that's all it costs, folks! Take your time there, folks, don't climb over each other! There's no rush! She's not going anywhere! Ever!"

She's inches away, but he's screaming again. Her face is still and flat, like a painting. He feels like slapping it. But doesn't. Because as fast as it came, it's gone now, the rage, like a summer squall. In times to come he will remember the raw feelings of the previous minute, not the words.

She hasn't moved. Still she stands before him with the goofy hat over her ears. She's stopped crying. She reaches up to the hat and pulls out the yellow feather and hands it to him and walks away.

But he's not finished. There's one more thing. His best shot. Then it will be over. She's moved away, but he speaks as if she's right beside him. He takes a breath. This was easier when he was screaming. "You used to be great, Becca Finch. Funny. Sweet. Lovable. Now you're dead. Big deal.

Get over it. Get a life. Get a death. Whatever. This is *your* forever you're missing."

She continues walking. Did she hear him?

Now she stops, in a cluster of mitteny sassafras. Her shoulders hunch, her hands go to her face. "Oh my God," he hears. "I had it backward. It's not about you. It never has been. I'm not here for you." She turns to face him. "*You're* here for *me*."

A faint smile appears on her face, and he knows, yes, that is the truth of it. They stand simply, totally, looking at each other across the sassafras and ferns. Worm has been to church. He has a sense of the word *sacred*. There are no stained-glass windows here, only sweet roots and spiders and a river you can jump across, but he knows he is in no less a sacred place. He is inside a prayer.

Neither moves. This is the closest they will ever be again. "Becca—" he says, but is stayed by her raised finger. She removes the goofy hat and Frisbees it to him perfectly. He snatches it from the air. She blows him a kiss. He pretends to catch it and plants it on his nose. She laughs. She turns and walks. He knows she will not stop, so he must say it now and hope forever. He calls: "Becca . . . you were a girl in love! I forgive you! The fireflies forgive you! Forgive yourself!"

He watches as she walks through the trees and the pooling shadows until she is gone.

He begins to walk in that direction. Stops. No. There is no following her.

A flare of raspberry in a patch of mayapples. A slipper. Only one. He knows it was no accident. He runs the fluff against his cheek. Now they've each got one.

In time he turns to go home. The brook is playing a song he will forever associate with her. The sun has set. Night has begun.

The fireflies are out.

THURSDAY

Worm knows it's coming.

The second Eddie sits down beside him on the bus: "Where were you?"

Worm has thought about it. Obviously, he can't tell him the truth. But lying has problems too. Eddie knows him so well, he's hard to sneak a lie past. So he decides to go with vague and hope Eddie backs off. "I got sidetracked."

Eddie looks like he's never even heard the word. "Sidetracked? What's that mean?"

Worm shrugs, tries to look no-big-dealish. "Other stuff to do. Fish to fry."

"Fish to fry? What fish? What're you talking about?" Apparently, Eddie isn't big on metaphor. "Important enough fish to keep you from the fight? I kept looking for ya."

"I wasn't there."

"Yeah, that's the point. You weren't there. Where . . . Hey"—he pokes Worm in the shoulder—"I heard you fainted in Language Arts. What's *that* about?"

"I didn't eat breakfast. Big mistake."

"Girls faint," says Eddie. "Guys don't faint."

"I guess I'm a girl, then," says Worm. Eddie gives him a look like Worm's a hard question on a test. Worm grabs the chance to shed the spotlight. "So how was the fight?" Worm really couldn't care less, but he's surprised there's been no buzz about it on the bus.

Eddie snorts. "There was no fight."

"Huh?"

"Everybody showed but Snake."

"You're kidding. All that buildup."

"Cross my heart." He crosses his heart.

Now that Worm thinks about it, when he saw Jeep in the hallway yesterday morning, he already looked ready to kill somebody. Snake? Worm never did see Snake. Maybe he never even showed up for school.

"Everybody was there," says Eddie. "Even girls. Jeep was bonzo, challenging guys to fight. Nobody was dumb enough to step up. Then two girls—Patti Calucci and Joanne Hertz—started smacking each other—"

"Who?" says Worm.

"Patti Calucci and Joanne Hertz—until Patti ran home crying. So it wasn't a *total* loss."

There's really only one school thing that interests Worm. If this was yesterday, he wouldn't have the nerve to say it. But now it's Becca's voice in his ear: *Be bold, Worm.*

"So Bijou . . . ," he says. "Did you make your move?"

Eddie studies the passing scenery out the window. "Nah," he says finally. "I decided to let her stew for a couple days. Build up the pressure. By the time I do it, she'll be panting with her tongue hanging out."

When Bijou boards the bus, her tongue seems to be pretty much in place. This time she doesn't do her usual aisle walk. She stands the rest of the way. The bus driver lets her. She doesn't turn. She doesn't smile at anybody.

Before homeroom is over, the truth tidal-waves over the whole school. Eddie made his move, all right. And she said no. *No!*

Santa Claus. Dumped.

Easter Bunny. Dumped.

Eddie Fusco. Dumped.

What can you trust anymore?

Worm hardly slept last night. But he's not tired. In fact, he's wound up. But there's nothing to do about it. Well, except for one thing, but that will have to wait till next week.

Meanwhile, as he moves from class to class through the school day, he scans for signs that someone else had an experience like his, that he's not the only one. It's not easy. What would such a sign look like? Haunted eyes? Dazed? It could be anything, really, different from the usual. (He wonders how he looks to others. So far nobody has said anything, unless you count Eddie on the bus.)

He inspects everyone. And everybody but one appears ordinary, disappointingly themselves. As if yesterday never happened. The sole exception is a shocker: Mean Monica Biddle. She's created a minor sensation by wearing her black shirt again today. Everyone else has turned them in. (Those who didn't trash theirs yesterday.) She wears it all day. She takes the mocking—there's a lot of it—with a surprising smile. But even the mockers get the point: the Wrappers—no, scrap that word—the victims, their dead age-mates, deserve more than one day's recognition, more than a hundred name cards and pictures tossed in trash cans and headed for the landfill.

Mean Monica complicates his feelings. On the one hand, he feels like saluting her for having the guts to do what nobody else would do. On the other hand, he can't help wondering if and how her doing double black-shirt duty plays into the declaration on the bus that day over a year ago: "Get a life, Worm."

Before then she was, well, a little more than just another girl. A member of the Bijou-Claire group. Boy haters until about sixth grade, except that with Monica and Worm there was an unexpected twist. She didn't seem to hate him. On occasion she actually spoke to Worm. Usually just a "Hi," but that's all it took to make her stick out. She seemed to get a kick out of saying his name. She'd make her voice low and go, "Hello, Mr. . . . *Worrrrm.*" (He got a kick out of that but of course didn't show it, as he was a normal girl-hating boy.) Once, she made a big deal of stepping around him. "Don't wanna squash you," she said, and giggled. If he had to describe her in those grade school days, he might have said "funny."

Like that, until about the time when all the other girls stopped ignoring boys—which was when Monica *started* ignoring him. And sometime later, for reasons still unknown, she made the bus declaration and hasn't spoken to him since. (Well, except after the fainting thing yesterday.)

And now he's got Becca Finch saying, "This is your life you're missing." And it annoys the crap out of him that Becca would say practically the same thing Mean Monica has been saying for over a year. And he wonders how two girls he feels so differently about can have the same view of him.

Monica's black shirt seems to have no effect on Claire Meeson, who's gabbing away with Monica as usual before Language Arts begins. And Monica must know that Claire, who's nice to everybody, makes no exception of Worm, even speaks to and smiles at him. So how come Mean Monica hasn't contaminated Claire with Worm hate?

Complicated.

At least twenty times during the day, Worm glances at his wrist, only to find that's all there is: wrist, no watch. If Worm was a puppy out for a walk, time would be his leash, lashing him to the world. He keeps feeling not so much free as lost, forced to forfeit the prime parameter of his life and just . . . romp. But he's never been a romper. Which may be, along with her own reasons, why Becca buried the watch.

Anyway, from last night until he left for school today, he had to fight the temptation to rush into the woods and dig it up. But he didn't. He tries mightily to not look as often as he usually does at the classroom clocks. Hey, she changed (he thinks, hopes). Why can't he?

It is the second-strangest day of his life. All day—in hall-ways, classrooms, lunchroom, stairways, even the boys' room—his peripheral vision is on high alert, ready for the briefest flash of raspberry. He stops at the water fountain—*Move it, sonny*—drinks long, hoping. He goes to the boys' room three times. The third time he sneaks down to the auditorium, finds the same seat, imagines her onstage, bowing to the audience—*Thank you . . . thank you . . . you're too kind.* He hears again the song she wrote, feels it below the land of words, finds himself crying again. . . . *Let's blow this dump.*

He barely survived Language Arts. *Oh boy. I was afraid of this.*

He shuns the bus, walks home. Makes a point of walking past the Play It Again Sam thrift shop . . . Dollar General . . . the beech tree. Considers doing the park, decides to save it for later. Finds the gardenia house. Picks one. Smells it. Smells her.

To please his mother, he eats a little dinner. Then into the woods, where he wanders . . . wanders. Dips his hand in the running water, in the mud. Pulls a sassafras root, inhales its root beer scent.

In his room he is by the window long after his parents have gone to bed. The light is out. The night outside is twinkling with fireflies. *I thought the stars had come down.* He does not know what time he goes to bed. He's turned the alarm clock facedown on the bedside table.

When he closes his eyes, he brings the pillow to his face and kisses it long and sweet, reliving.

THE FIRST DAY OF
SUMMER VACATION

What rotten luck.

This is what Worm gets for ignoring his bike for so long: a half-flat back tire.

If it's a leak, he prays it's a slow one.

He finds the ancient hand pump, cobwebby in a corner of the toolshed. Takes off the air cap. Screws on the pump hose nozzle. Straddles the pump on its flat metal feet. Starts pumping.

He makes the tire as hard as he dares. Listens. No hiss. Tops off the front tire too.

Shakes the seat. The bottle, duct-taped to the seat bottom, doesn't flinch.

No cell phone. No distractions.

He's good to go.

*   *   *

The map is folded in his pocket. He looked up *eastern Pennsylvania road map* on his mom's laptop and printed it out. Most of it is along Route 6.

At first he figured 15 mph, then remembered where he was. Hello? ... Pocono *Mountains*? So: 10 mph. He ballparked one-way bike time at four to six hours. But who knows? Factor in the time he spends there—another unknown—and the return time. He's lied to his parents, said he'll be gone "all day," intends to "start out early." What else can he do? So here he is, coasting down the driveway at 6:00 a.m.—as in *morning*—and all he can do now is hope he makes it back home before his parents call the cops. Well, that and avoid becoming eighteen-wheeler roadkill.

It shocks him how quickly he finds himself in territory he doesn't recognize. Bumps are rocky. But the tire is holding, which is good. He feels beneath the seat. The bottle is tight.

He keeps looking at his right wrist, where his watch used to be. He wonders if it's still ticking away in its little grave hole, annoying some ants. Or worms. Each day so far he's asked himself: *Shall I dig it up?* Each day the answer's been the same: *Not yet.*

Left onto Hummels Hill.

Plowed fields. Something green coming up. Corn? He

prefers white corn over yellow. Slathered with butter, heavy on the salt and pepper.

Handmade sign: COUNTRY BREAD. Arrow pointing down a long, graveled driveway.

He wonders how long he's been gone. It feels like two hours, but he suspects it's less than fifteen minutes. Each day he seems to miss his watch less.

Left on Gwendolyn.

He was deliberately vague with his parents about his travels today. At first he was going to say he was riding with Eddie—which they always do, first day of vacation—but then thought better of it. Just his luck that Eddie would call their landline—after trying Worm's cell and getting no answer because it's in his room buzzing—and his mother answers, and he asks for Worm, and his mother goes into shock and says, "Robbie? Isn't he with *you*?" So: vague.

Which doesn't mean Eddie isn't on his mind. As always, Eddie unfolds Worm's mind like a cheap tent chair and plops it down whenever he pleases. Only now it's not Eddie sitting in it. It's Becca.

At graduation everybody was watching Eddie and Bijou. Hoping for drama, fireworks, something. Nothing happened. As far as anyone could tell, they never even looked at each other. Meanwhile, Eddie has already been seen snoogling up to Karen Deloplaine, the field hockey star.

Worm has to hand it to Eddie. He's always in the center of the field, never on the sidelines. He doesn't think. He doesn't wait. He *does*.

Right on Moonjack Road.

Worm at graduation? Hugs from lots of girls, a couple he doesn't even know. Long one from Claire Meeson. Not Mean Monica, of course. But one surprising thing: as she was talking excitedly with Bijou and other girls, a sudden shift of the eyes, visible to Worm even across the courtyard. Just a second, then back to the girls. The eyes could have been aiming anywhere, but for some brainless reason he decided they were aimed at him—until he remembered he's not exactly great with eyes, remembered he once thought (actually believed) that Beautiful Bijou Newton sent him a love-struck look on the bus on Dead Wednesday.

Whatever, Worm was surprised to discover that a shift of two eyes can make him feel good. The moment returned him to a probably dumb question he's had now and then: By the very act of not looking at or speaking to him, has Mean Monica been trying to tell him something? It's at times like this that Worm totally gets what Eddie often says: "You think too much."

Right on Dorchester.

The zone he's been in since she walked into the green and shadows—there is no name for it. There is no vocabulary for the things that happened last Wednesday. Language dams feeling's flow, names it, shapes it. Without words, he finds for the first time in his life something that is hard, if not impossible, to think about. And yet it is all there, inside him, filling him like air in a leakless tire. He *feels* it, and the feeling is better than thinking, better than words. He's tried a number of them. *Ghost* doesn't even come close. Neither does *spirit* or *soul* or *angel.* Becca. That's all. *Becca.*

Ah . . . Route 6. Amosland Pike in these parts.

Anyway, having no words is no problem. Words are to communicate, and he has no intention of ever telling anybody what happened. Pedaling, he amuses himself by scripting imaginary conversations between himself and Eddie.

Worm: *You remember my Dead Wednesday card? The girl? Becca Finch?*

Eddie: *I just remember seeing it. Don't remember the picture. I'd remember if she was hot.*

Worm: *I met her.*

Eddie: *You already knew her? From before?*

Worm: *No. After.*

Eddie: *After what?*

Worm: *After she died.*

Eddie: *After she* died?

Worm: *Yep.*

Now comes the best part. Because at first Eddie is ready to laugh or smirk—like, *Yeah, right.* But now he sees the look on Worm's face and he knows—he *knows*—Worm is not messing with him, and, incredibly, Eddie Fusco looks lost.

This is Worm's favorite version, as long as it ends right there. Because when he strings it out further—which he loves, he loves telling Eddie everything his feeble words will allow, her goofy ways, the hat, the pj's, the kisses—Eddie always responds by shaking his head sadly and saying something like, *Really, Worm? You're so hard up now you're* making up *girls?* And always ends with Eddie's favorite word, for the first time ever aimed at his best pal: *Pathetic.*

Spooling miles on his spinning pedals. He passes a sign:

ELWOOD 27

From the moment he turned and walked back through the woods, back home, he was pretty sure he would never see her again, though for years he won't be able to drink from a water fountain without looking up. More generally, he doubts he will ever understand How It All Works. But so what? She doesn't know either. Yet there she was. Is.

So he's left with nothing but himself. Himself and a wordless memory. He knew he had to *do* something. And then immediately knew what that something must be. He must go to her. The mortal remains of her. The cemetery. Except for the bottle, he doesn't know what he'll do when he gets there, but be there he must. Gravity: he is an apple falling toward Elwood.

He has already googled her. Got himself a Facebook page and checked out hers. Was cryingly thankful it hadn't been taken down. She didn't post a lot. More pictures of other people than herself. The heartbreaker was a shot of her and Pooter. It was a selfie, him and her, cheek to cheek, mugging goofily into the camera. With Pooter's face all crunchy, Worm couldn't tell if he was as beautiful as Becca said. He wished it could always have been like that, fun.

As he pedals, he thinks of other things he could do. Get a look at her school. Her house and family. Waldo's. Whatever has replaced the crashed car. Pooter. Walk the route from her house to school. Get *Wendy Wins*. Read it. New things keep occurring to him. He can see himself making a pilgrimage to Elwood every week—month?—for the rest of his life.

ELWOOD 12

He feels for the bottle. He got it at Acme. Expected to get a soda bottle, but they were all plastic. So it's Heinz apple cider vinegar. He emptied out the vinegar down the sink and chucked the cap.

Pedal . . . pedal . . .

On the map it's only a couple of inches.

The plan came to him over the weekend. He will smash

197

the bottle against her tombstone. He knows it sounds weird, and if he has to, he'll pedal to Elwood a hundred times till he can do it without being seen. He knows it's just a futile, symbolic gesture and hopes/suspects/prays that she's free from the bottle anyway. He's doing this for himself, he understands that. But then again . . .

He keeps reminding himself: he doesn't *know* How It All Works, so if there's a one-in-a-trillion chance . . .

Eddie remains, and probably always will remain, the only other person he's shown Becca's card to. Every day he replays the scene on the stairwell, Eddie all proud, showing him the picture of his gorgeous dead girl, Kat—then barely glancing at Becca and writing her off with a sniffy "Not impressed."

He's passing a roadside fruit stand now. Long Old West dresses, gauzy caps: Mennonites. He waits till he's past the stand and shouts it across the truck-roaring mountains: "Well, I am!"

ELWOOD 2

Long uphill here. He feels the gust of a passing truck. His calves feel like bricks, not achy, just pumping away, like his heart, banging on his ribs like it wants to get out. He knows it's not just about the hill.

He's happy to note that the obsessive question that

hounded him for days—*Am I crazy?*—is receding. What's surprising is the reason why: there's no need for an answer. It makes no difference. It's neither yes nor no. He had an experience and it was real for him and that's that. For all he knows, people all over the world are having similar experiences and, like him, they can't talk about them. Nobody would understand. Or believe.

Worm-word-wise, there's been no eruption since The Day. If his raging outburst came as a surprise to Becca, it did not surprise him. The inside of his head has heard rants like that for years. The difference since Wednesday? The words are coming out. Not rants, just regular talk, and not just with Eddie. And more than once he's caught himself being the first to speak.

Every night and sometimes in the morning, Worm reaches into the back of his closet and touches them: the raspberry fluffie and the floppy, yellow-feathered sombrero. Quite a few times already he has seen his mother—in the garden, bringing apron pocketfuls of string beans into the kitchen—wearing her featherless, floppy hat, making of herself, in Worm's eyes, someone she will never know: sister to a dead girl.

And something else happens at random moments during the day, something he cannot touch or pick up yet feels no less, a memory that his body feels now, pedaling, a week later: the weight of her—the sheer, human, earthly *weight* of her—sitting on his lap in his father's pickup.

And here we are:

YOU ARE ENTERING
ELWOOD

He knows where to go. Down the main street, Willard. Through town. The usual stuff: stores, traffic lights, people. Left on Persimmon. Down a ways . . . on the right . . . and here it is. Fair Acres. Shabby sign. Needs painting. One of his trips here, he's going to bring paint and brush, do it himself.

He stops inside the entrance. He refolds the route map and returns it to his pocket, where it joins her Dead Wednesday card. He carries it everywhere he goes, intends to wrap it in plastic. He could have printed out the cemetery map, the layout of grave sites, but he memorized it, wanted it in his head, part of himself. It would be insulting to need a map to find her. Her grave is on Westview Drive.

He starts to pedal. Stops. Needs to calm down. All that riding and *now* he's out of breath. A sudden percolation of doubts. Last Wednesday was something that *happened* to him. Now it's him driving the bus. Is he intruding? Messing with How It All Works? Should he turn and go home?

"Worm."

He laughs out loud. . . . No, he didn't really hear her whisper his name, but his ever-clever mind went movie scene and—*ka-ching*—whispered it into his ear. And in the process breaks the tension and, doubts begone, he knows he belongs here as much as anybody. He locates Westview and slowly cruises the winding way, a feeling of her—*Becca*—getting stronger and stronger as he closes in.

And here it is. Her stone.

High as his waist. White marble, looks like. Rounded top.

He stops. Is suddenly afraid to come closer. He reads the chiseled figures:

REBECCA ANN FINCH

BELOVED DAUGHTER

NOVEMBER 1, 2003–DECEMBER 24, 2020

Sitting on his parked bike, no more than ten feet from the stone, he realizes that the sense of her—her *presence*—has fled. So powerful, so *personal*, was his experience last Wednesday that this—a *stone*—leaves him deflated, empty. Whatever may be here, it's no match for the Becca Finch who sat on his lap. He knows now he will never make this trip again.

He dismounts. He unfastens the vinegar bottle from under the seat. He's expected this moment to be so powerful, if only symbolic. Now it feels silly, vandal-like. But he feels bound to go through with it. He steps up to the marble marker, goes around to the faceless back so as not to disturb the lettering, and without ceremony whips the bottle against the stone.

He tries to convince himself that he hears a smashing-glass echo somewhere in the afterlife. Yeah, and camels speak French.

"What's going on?"

He's never heard the voice before, but he knows who it is before he looks up. Pooter. As beautiful as Becca said. Dusty-pink polo. Gray cargo pants. Linebacker legs.

"Hi," says Worm brilliantly.

"What's going on?" says Pooter, taking a step forward. No car is visible nearby. Does he walk here every day?

"I came to visit," says Worm. "The grave."

"Becca? You knew her? Who are you?"

He should have been ready for this.

"Yeah, our families were friends. Going way back. They would come see us. We used to talk. Me and Becca."

"Where you from?"

Not Amber Springs. "Scranton."

"What's your name?"

"Wor—uh—Robbie."

"Robbie what?" He takes another step forward. He's looking at the ground.

"Johnson," he says. Lying is exhausting.

"What's all this glass?"

"Yeah," says Worm, "that's what I was wondering. I got here and this is what I found. Figured I'd start picking it up."

Pooter stares at him, skeptical. He looks back at the bike. "You came on *that*?"

How far is Scranton? "Yeah. Started out early. First day of vacation, y'know?"

"All this way? Bike?" Skeptical.

"Yeah," says Worm. Deals a little chuckle and nod, like, *I know what you mean.* "Wasn't sure I could make it. Lotsa hills."

And suddenly Pooter is here, towering over him, his shoes crunching glass. "I never heard her mention you, you're such old pals. Robbie . . ."

"Johnson."

"Johnson." He looks around the cemetery. He's standing with his arm touching the stone. He looks Worm up and down. "You didn't bike here from Scranton."

Change the game. "She talked about you all the time . . . Pooter."

That gets his attention. He boggles. His lips falter. The glare is gone. But only for a moment. He recovers with a face harder than ever. He's mad. Worm said the wrong thing. He gives Worm a shoulder shove. "You're lying." For Pooter, Becca stops at the end of what he knows. "How do you know my name?"

Spill it and scram. *Be bold.*

"She babysat me when I was little. We texted a lot. Especially about you. Harmon Dean Baker. She named you Pooter. You met at Waldo's. 'Thank you, good sir,' she said when you opened the door."

He's backed off but still fighting it. "You weren't at the funeral."

"I was sick. The flu. We all stayed home."

Pooter starts shoeing pieces of glass into a pile. He looks at the bike, shakes his head. "No way. From Scranton?"

"I was up before the sun. No stops to eat."

So much . . . so much Worm wants to tell him, complete the Becca picture for him, but he can't. He imagines the day after Christmas, the Baker family pulling into the driveway, the snow in the front yard smooth, undisturbed. It's killing him to not say what her plans were, her mission to delight him with the snow-dug double-heart emoji, the duct tape. But something wiser than himself is telling him to leave it be. It would be wrong to give Pooter a memory he doesn't already have. He could never own it.

Worm has already said too much. And Pooter is letting him off the hook. He knows Worm did not bike here from Scranton. He knows Worm had something to do with the broken glass. He knows Worm is not telling him every-thing.

And Worm? Worm knows this is *their* place, Pooter and Becca's. He does not belong here.

"Well," he says, trying to act casual, "better be going. Long ride back." He holds out his hand. "Nice to meet you, Pooter."

At this point they are on opposite sides of the stone, as Worm has been edging toward his parked bike. His out-stretched hand hangs in the air over the still-new marble arch.

By now Pooter has the glass footed into a pile. Where's a dustpan when you need one? In time Pooter looks up, dis-covers the hand hanging over the gravestone. He stares at it. He seems to be deciding something. At last he reaches out and shakes Worm's hand. When Worm pulls away, Pooter's hand stays behind, resting on the top of the stone.

Worm has a thought that never would have occurred to him before last Wednesday: if there's anything left to be said to Pooter, Becca will find a way.

He pedals off.

It's all changed. He's lost his appetite for drama. He will never look for her house. Whatever eternity has in store for her, Worm will play no part.

And he's OK with that. Pooter is the rightful custodian of her memory. The relief Worm feels now tells him he got out just in time. He stops at the Mennonite fruit stand, treats himself to a massive chocolate-covered strawberry.

He smiles as he rides, thinking of them. A sweet feeling is rising in him, and it surprises him to realize what it is: pride. He's proud of Pooter. He wasn't exactly chummy with Worm, but Worm could see the quality. Six months later and he still visits the grave every day; Worm is sure of it. And Becca—he couldn't be prouder if she was his sister. He's proud to have known them both. What a couple they must have been!

There's plenty of daylight left on this Wednesday in June, but there's plenty of road left too. He picks up the pace, dares to race the sun—for a reason that's new to him. He wishes he brought his phone. He would like to call his parents, tell them not to worry, he's OK.

THE FOURTH OF JULY

They walk. Worm. Eddie.

Usually for a distance like this they would bike. Worm sleeps over so often at Eddie's that he has a junker backup stashed in his best pal's toolshed.

But not today.

Per tradition, they walk all the way from Eddie's house to the park. Because on this day, walking the town is part of the deal. It's the little kids. Usually invisible to teenagers, on this day, suddenly, here they are, taking over the place, going batso wherever you look: running, screaming, waving flags and sparklers, tooting kazoos, croaking noisemakers, banging pans. There's a manic look in their eyes. Maybe they're making up for not being allowed to stay up till midnight on New Year's Eve.

And yet it's not just spectator fun for Worm, not like

the other years. He finds himself on edge, afraid one of the little kids will dash into a street, into a car. He's alert, poised to spring if he has to.

Along the way they collect Otter and two others: posse. Otter, as always on this day, is decked out in a red-white-and-blue stovepipe hat. Hardly a minute goes by that some little kid doesn't try to knock the hat from his head. They jump, grunting, but they're too short. It only gets worse at the park, already bustling. Before you can smell the first hot dog, Otter lifts one little kid up so he can knock off the hat. Makes the little kid's year.

Fourth of July at the park is a ten-ring circus. By mid-afternoon the whole town will be here. Sack races. Egg toss. Frisbee Frolic. Magicians. Until the talent show officially begins, the band shell stage and microphone are available to anyone wanting to star in Amber Springs Has Talent. A policeman stands in the wings.

Somebody is reading a poem. The voice sounds familiar. Worm looks. It's Claire Meeson. He only catches the second half of it, something about freedom and the price of tomatoes. He's shocked to see meek Claire Meeson performing onstage. Nobody but Worm is paying attention. Worm's not big on poetry and he has no idea if her poem is good or not, but at least she's up there, doing it. *You go, girl,* he thinks. She's barely finished the last word when she hustles off the stage. Worm feels rotten. He could have clapped—still could, not too late—but he'd be the only one, and of course he's too shy (OK, cowardly) for that. A little kid darts past the cop, yells, "Poop!" into the mic, and darts off. The cop laughs. People clap.

Grilling meat flavors the air. Every picnic table in the grove is taken. Folding tables, portable grills everywhere. Lines at Hickey's food stand.

And people. The whole town. Every couple seconds the posse bumps into other ASMS kids. High-fiving. Trash-talking. Mock fights. As always, Eddie leads the way, sets the agenda. "Let's do this." "Let's do that." Parents have stuffed their pockets with food money.

Waves of recently minted ninth graders, not to mention all the other grades, surge across ball fields, invade the playground, little kids waiting and scowling because hooting fourteen-year-olds are hogging the swings. The next time this many of them will be in the same place will be the first day of high school.

This year things are different. Well, not things. *Himself.* There's no way to document it, but he knows when it started. The day after The Day. Brushing his teeth. As usual, he did so without looking at himself in the mirror. Then, capping the toothpaste tube, he did—and discovered that the sight of his complexion left him . . . flat. He reached for the old familiar pain, the disgust, but it wasn't there. Hasn't been since.

211

You have good bones.

On the Friday after The Day, he went back into the woods, all the way to the brook. He searched for a daddy longlegs but couldn't find one. But he did find mitten-shaped sassafras leaves. One of these days he's going to make root beer. If it's good enough, maybe serve it to the writers. Since then, toeing over rocks, he's found half a dozen salamanders. Once, he shouted. No particular words. Just shouted in the woods. Another day, after Elwood, he got out the old hand pump and pumped air into the perfectly fine back tire of his bike. The tire got hard as a rock, but he kept pumping . . . and pumping. In time a black bubble of inner tube peeked out like a tongue from between tire and rim. The bubble went from black to gray as it got fatter and fatter—and finally popped in a rubbery gust of bad breath. It felt good to do something stupid.

By now he knows he'll never dig up the watch.

They're starting the egg toss in the outfield of the American Legion baseball field. He breaks from the posse and says, "Who's coming with me?" Eddie looks at him like, *Do I know you?* But Otter, bless him, rams the second half of a hot dog into his mouth and glubbles, "Yez doot."

They're one of half a hundred teams, three-year-olds

to old farts. They're instructed to face each other nose to nose. Grinning, Otter leans—he's taking the command literally, too close for Worm's comfort—but Worm inches up to Otter's nose and bumps it with his own. Now they're instructed to each take one step back. Somebody hands Worm an egg, brown. The guy with the megaphone goes, "Toss!" and Worm tosses the egg to Otter. Otter's hands receive it softly, giving with the incoming arc of the egg. Worm, well known as a klutz, tries to emulate Otter. He doesn't, but at least the egg doesn't break. He notices that some people have come prepared: they're wearing aprons.

Back a step—toss. Back a step—toss. Splats, shrieks: teams are leaving the field. Worm has had fun before, but never this *kind* of fun. He's thinking maybe he'll try out for JV soccer next year. With each step back Otter whispers, "Easy, Worm . . . soft hands." They're at least ten steps apart (Worm can't believe he's this good; maybe they got a hard-boiled egg) when it happens—*splat!*—yellowy mess on his hands, shirt, yolk and shell shrapnel rolling down the front of his pants. He scoops off what he can, wipes his hands on the grass. Otter is cracking up. As they leave the field, a little kid high-fives them both.

The next event is always a crowd favorite: the Great Foamalooza. The fire trucks are ready. People in bathing suits are rushing to the soccer field. Most are little kids, of course, but there are more than a couple of teens in there too, girls and boys, and one wrinkly old lady, prompting Eddie to clap his hand over his eyes and go, "I can't take it!"

Fire truck bells clang and out comes the foam, and within a minute a hundred deliriously dancing humans are awash in bubbles. "Whoa!" goes Otter, and nobody has to ask who he's spotted. It's Beautiful Bijou, in an aqua two-piece. Worm's not sure if it qualifies as a bikini, but who cares? Worm resists the urge to look at Eddie, see if he's reacting. Bijou is twirling and slinging foam with other girls, one of whom, Worm notices, seems to be Monica Biddle. But maybe not. Bathing suit (definitely two-piece, off-white), wet hair, so un–Mean Monica–like as she dances and laughs and frolics: hard to believe.

So goes the day. The posse joins a thousand others at the bandstand, enduring the off-key singers, the occasional surprise ("Whoa! Who is *that*?") of the annual talent show, no cop needed now. By the show's halfway mark, the posse has had enough. They take off, except for Worm, who says, "Go ahead. I'm staying. I'll find yas." He's thinking of the remaining contestants, somewhere backstage, maybe peeking around a corner. He doesn't want them to see him leaving, whoever they are, turning his back on them.

He understands, at least as the guys see it, he's veer-

214

ing from the old Worm. But, like the face in the mirror, he doesn't care. Occasionally he's caught Eddie looking at him funny, once muttering, "Worm, *what?*"

Every so often he has allowed himself to feel good about what he hopes he did for her. But these days he's more occupied with a transition of his own, from her to the gifts she left him with.

Which doesn't mean she's not with him, even on this tumultuous day. It happens both when he's with the posse and when he's not. For a flicker of a moment . . . *maybe?* A glimpse of blondish hair. A flash of raspberry. A moonwalker in the foam. A shouted name: "Rebecca!" It never turns out to be her, of course, but he can't help checking.

The crowds, if anything, get even bigger as dusk approaches. The word *fireworks* is seldom heard, yet from the first kazoo when they stepped out of Eddie's house, every minute of the day has been draining toward the final glimmer of daylight. Families spread blankets over the vast, grassy banks surrounding the American Legion baseball field. Little kids have made the leap beyond mere excitement. They can barely be spoken to, directed. They are in the land of puppies.

All day long eyes have drifted toward the infield, scarcely believing that tonight's magic is, for the moment, packed into the black tubes poking out of the sandy soil. The sight always makes Worm think of whisker stubble on the chin of a giant.

The trees beyond the dugouts fling their shadows from third base to left field, minute by minute dissolving into the darkening dusk. The posse finds a spot, by instinct roosting among others of their kind, Amber Springs teenagers.

The murmuring din of thousands becomes louder and louder, more highly charged, as if a great knob somewhere is being turned up, until . . .

Whump!

Sudden silence. The first warning cannon-shot has been fired. Ten thousand upward eyes follow a missile they cannot see, which abruptly crashes upon the sky, spilling a gorgeous downpour of gold and a crinkle of stars over the infield.

Otter cries out: "It's on!"

The night explodes in geysers of color. Worm lounges back on his elbows, wonder-struck at the spectacle like everyone else. He cheers with everyone else when a stray gob of red falls upon a fire truck. When a firefly twinkles past his nose, it takes him a beat to react. He sits up, scans, locates it winking over the people's heads, right before their eyes, yet no one seems to see it, such are the marvels in the sky.

Worm does not realize he's standing until he feels slaps on his shins, tugs on his pants.

Eddie barks: "Worm!"

Others chime in:

"Down in front!"

"Sit!"

"I'll putcha down!"

He alone is standing among the five thousand. Now he is walking, the front of him lit red beneath a shower of pomegranate pearls. He is moving generally in the direction of the firefly, picking his way among the bodies on the ground. He's not sure where he is going or why, only that things are coming together on another field and he must leave the sideline. The faces, so many faces, marveling in the splashing lights . . . her whisper in his ear: *Be bold, Worm.*

He finds himself passing a cluster of girls, their faces strobing on and off with the stutter of the skylight. It's his classmates. He spots Beautiful Bijou—defoamed, dry, and back to normal—and Claire Meeson and Mean Monica, and he sees the heavens celebrate in the reflecting eyes of every girl, and it's coming together . . . coming together. . . .

Be bold, Worm.

And he feels it . . . a word . . . a name . . . in his mouth . . . leaning on his lips. . . .

Get a life, Worm.

And he does it, he lets the name out: "Monica."

In a world visible only to Worm, the rockets halt half-way to the sky, the raining colors freeze as if snapshot. All the girls before him, all five thousand faces, are focused on the halted rockets. All except one. Monica Biddle turns her eyes from the sky to the voice that uttered her name, and when they land on him . . . well . . . he knows for sure this time who they're looking at. Her face is surprise. Her face is question. And now her face is level with his, because she is standing among her sitting girlfriends and the night is exploding again and he and Monica Biddle are the only two standing, looking at each other across a painting of faces that has returned to animated rapture.

She's moving, weaving through the bodies until she's right up to him, close. "What?" she says.

He has no words prepared, yet here they are: "There's a better show."

She nods. "OK."

He knows she must have been cute for the past year, but he's just seeing it now. He turns and starts walking, feels her following, hears the calls:

"Monnie! Get back here!"

"Go, girl!"

In the strobing light they pick their way through the crowd, up the long slope to the boulevard, walking side by side, saying nothing.

He knows now where they're going. Well, not the coordinates maybe, but the *kind* of place. He'll know it when he sees it. They walk. Two kids walking down the boulevard at night, behind them the boom and clatter of the fireworks receding. Until the grand finale, thirty seconds of reward for a year of waiting, a volley of cannon-shot and screaming sky that must be visible from Saturn. Neither one turns around to look.

The town is silent, deserted. But won't be for long; the crowd will be streaming back home.

He's looking . . . looking . . . and realizes as they turn from the park boulevard and head into the West End over the stone creek bridge and the tracks of the long-gone freight line that since they started walking, neither of them has said a word. The intensity of their mingled presences packs the air around them; there's no room for words.

One of his first memories comes to him. He'd never had a sister for reference, so one day—he couldn't have been more than three—he asked his mother what the difference is between boys and girls. He wishes he could go back in time now and see the look on her face as she answered his question. The difference, she said, basically has to do with books and comes into play once you go to school, especially by the time you hit middle school. Boys, she said, carry their books from class to class with one arm. The arm curls around the stack and clamps it to the hip. Girls, on the other hand, carry their books in front of them, cradling them against their bosom. At least that's how it used to be, she said, before backpacks.

Worm's not sure how long he continued to believe that, but he's pretty sure it was a lot longer than a couple of days.

And now, as they pass the abandoned asbestos factory, he needs to speak. "I used to call you Mean Monica," he says.

She laughs. "I know."

He's surprised. "How?"

She shoulder-bumps him. "Worm, duh, word gets around."

"Well," he says, "sorry. Like I said, '*used* to.'"

She laughs again, reminds him of someone else who laughs a lot. "Because of that time, right? When I told you to get a life?"

"Yeah," he says. "There's a fantasy. I imagine I'm a worm—"

She interrupts: "You *are* a worm."

"You gonna let me finish?"

She mock-bows. "My apologies. By all means, continue."

He tells her his Worm-up-her-nose fantasy. "The best part is when it happens at the dinner table. In front of your parents."

She's properly repelled. "Eww!" Then jumps from horror to grammar. "*Happens?* Present tense? You *still* do?"

"Oh, no . . ." He reaches out, touches her. She's looking

shocked and hurt and mad all at once, and he can't tell if any of it is serious. "Really . . . not anymore."

She lets herself be persuaded. And now she straightens her spine and puts on a sniffy air. "Well, I for one did not *fantasize* anything. I stuck *real* crayons up my *real* nose."

He loves it. "Impressive."

"And out of my ears! And guess how old I was."

"Three."

"Ten!"

They crack up, wobble, stagger until, blind with laughter, they bonk foreheads.

He's always been content to watch others be silly, mindless, childish. He never knew it feels so good. It occurs to him to tell her his mother's early definition of boys versus girls, then decides to hold it for next time. *Next time.* He already knows that sleep tonight will have to contend with laying out plans for next time.

"When I was three, I used to sing 'I'm a Little Teapot.'"

She stops, backs off. She bends her body into a pouring teapot. "This too? The whole thing?"

He pours himself. "The whole thing. I used to do it every week."

"Did you have an audience?"

"Guaranteed," he says. "I live in a place for writers. They stay in cabins. They eat in my house."

"I know," she says. She's grinning.

221

"I could show you. It's out in the boondocks. I practically live in the woods."

"I love boondocks," she says.

"I walk in the woods. I let daddy longlegs crawl on me. I could show you salamanders. Did you know frying pans used to be called salamanders? I can make root beer from sassafras!"

He's not sure if he's impressed her speechless or if she's simply content to listen. In any case, she's still grinning and nodding with every revelation. What's the world coming to? Worm: Mr. Talky.

"Guess who I met a couple weeks ago?"

"Who?"

"Daisy Chimes."

That stops her cold. She boggles. "No way."

"Way," he says. "Ever read *Wendy Wins*?"

She screeches. "Is Bijou beautiful?" Sends him a doubtful look. "*You* read it."

"Will. Soon as I get it," he says.

He wishes he could show her Becca's signed copy.

"I have a cool hat. I think you'd like . . ."

And here it is. They've walked and talked right up to it. The empty lot at the corner of Swede and Birch. Weedy, scruffy, ugly even in the barely diluted darkness of a distant streetlight. It's perfect.

He takes her by the hand and leads her into the middle

of the lot. A bottle goes skittering, now a can. She doesn't resist, doesn't ask what's going on. Since he first had the idea, he's assumed he will introduce it, frame it, tell her the story. And now: *No. Say nothing. Leave it to her.*

And already she is running to the center of the lot, twirling, hands to the sky, shouting: "Fireflies!" She turns to him, arms, it seems, welcoming the world. "I've never seen so many."

And she runs to him, gracelessly plunges into him, has to steady him from falling. The delight, the wonder in her eyes, is something he's seen in only one other. "You said."

"What?" he says.

"There's a better show."

Yeah, he did, didn't he?

They wander hand in hand, wordlessly, through the dancing fireflies, Becca's fallen stars.

The old question comes, just barges through the magic and into his head. He knows this is the absolute worst possible time to ask.

And maybe the best.

With a prayer that he's not about to blow the whole thing, he says, "Can I ask you a question?"

She's been doing a skip step, like a little girl. Now she stops, plants herself in front of him, grins. "Took you a while."

He's baffled. "Huh?"

"Why did I say it, right? Tell you to get a life?"

Is she a mind reader? Are all girls? "Well . . . yeah."

"Well, no," she says, backing off. "Not until you tell *me* something."

A curveball. "Like what?" he says.

"Like . . ." In first grade he might have called the grin on her face naughty. "Something personal. Say something personal to me." She twirls once. "Take your time," and whirls off among the fireflies.

Is this a critical moment? Worm's not sure. He figures he better play it safe, embarrassing or not. Suddenly he finds her carefree romp annoying. "Are you gonna frolic or are you gonna listen?"

She stops abruptly, cups her ears with her hands (which he also finds annoying). He takes a deep breath. "I sweat easy. So I have Right Guard in my backpack."

His watch is buried in the woods, so he can't be sure, but he guesses it takes at least five minutes for her to stop laughing. When she does, it takes another minute or two to catch her breath and regain her balance. She steadies herself with a hand on his shoulder. "Oh man . . . oh man . . ." She looks at him, touches his face as if to confirm he's real. "I guess that sorta answers another question too. Deodorant in your backpack? I'd say you're ready for girls."

He's never thought of it that way. Becca . . . Monica . . . they seem to know him better than he knows himself. For sure he's learning one thing: making a girl laugh beats a winning game at *Nuke 'Em ALL Now!* any day. And girls—well, sure, they cry, but they're also really, *really* good at being happy.

She raps lightly on his forehead with her knuckle. "The unknowable Mr. Tarnauer. Keeper of all thoughts."

"So *my* question, please."

She claps her hands. "Ah yes—the question. The question that's been tormenting you forever."

How does she know that?

She puts a hand on each of his shoulders and pushes herself to her tiptoes and brings her mouth to his ear. He feels the tiny puff of each whispered word: "I got your attention, didn't I?"

The logic of it escapes him. Where's a girl ghost to consult when you need one? He'll work on it later. Meanwhile, he's not done. "Then you didn't talk to me for over a year. Didn't even *look* at me."

She stands down, takes a step back, looks surprised in a pleased sort of way. "You noticed? You cared?"

He feels himself maturing by the minute. New wisdom: one must be careful when talking to girls. He shrugs. How to put it? "It bothered me."

A big smile from her. Good answer.

She pokes him in the chest. "Well, here's some breaking news, you big dummy. There's one thing you were wrong about. I never let you see it, but believe me, you were being looked at."

And a year of annoyance and flusterment vanishes.

"And every time I *didn't* talk to you or *didn't* look at you, you noticed. Didn't you, Robbie Tarnauer?"

She'll call you Robbie.

"Well, yeah, but not in a good way. I mean, it made me not like you."

He's not sure how it happened, but he notices they are now very close to each other, all four hands holding, her face tilted up. She grins. "Really? You want to rephrase that?"

He understands he doesn't have to answer. He feels like he's been performing for her amusement.

Her hands have left his. They're on his chest now. A kiss is coming. He's known it for a while. But he's cool. He had a good teacher. But no hurry. He's discovering that talk—*talk*—can be a kiss of its own.

"I don't even know why I stood up. The guys told me to get down."

"But you didn't."

"I stayed up and walked till I came to you girls."

"So brave." She taps the tip of his nose with her finger. "In front of all those people."

"I didn't know what I was doing there."

"I did."

"I thought I was gonna say Claire Meeson."

"I didn't."

"I said you."

"You said me."

"I don't even know why."

Her whisper is conspiratorial: "I do."

Becca, you'd love this girl.

Her hands have moved up now. They're fearlessly cupping his cheeks, like it's just another normal face. "Robbie, Robbie, Robbie . . . ," she says, the breath-puffs of her words pre-kissing his lips, "where *have* you been?"

THANK YOU

When this writer needed help, there was little waiting for answers from Joan Biondi, Marisa DiNovis, Mike Donnelly, Molly Gentilini, Teresa Hoover, Angel James, Kathy James, Lana James, Leah James, Sean James, Bill Johnson, Ben Spinelli, Lonnie Stebbins, and Jean Szegedy.

Special tribute to the unsung heroes of publishing: copy editors. My hawkeyes were Erica Stahler, Lisa Leventer, Amy Schroeder, Artie Bennett, and Alison Kolani.

Most thankfully—and regretfully—my deepest appreciation to the teacher whose name and letter I've lost; she planted the seed.

And to the two wonder women who simply made this book better: my editor, Nancy Siscoe, who came to the parade, and my wife, Eileen.